MARRIED TO A DIRTY SOUTH BOSS

LATEASHA RANKIN

Cole Hart
SIGNATURE SERIES

Mailing List

To stay up to date on new releases, plus get information on contests, sneak peeks, and more,

Go To The Website Below...

WWW.COLEHARTSIGNATURE.COM

CHAPTER 1

*T*here were only five minutes left in class and they were starting to seem like the longest five minutes in history to Lailah as she sat listening to her professor go over their study guide for their upcoming final. Thankfully, because she was exempt from her other courses, her English class was the only course she had to study for and she was prepared to ace her exam with flying colors.

"Have a good afternoon," Professor Wrigley announced, finally wrapping up his lesson. "I'll see you all Monday."

Shit, finally. Lailah thought as she grabbed her purse, folder, and keys then rushed towards the door, joining her other classmates. She maneuvered through the student bodies then stepped into the crowded and noisy hallway. She had one thing on her mind, getting off campus then visiting her friend Janae for a little girl talk and bullshit. The light chirp from her phone indicated she had a message. She quickly pulled her phone from her back pocket, tapped the screen, and then entered her passcode, unlocking her device. She looked down at her phone and noticed that one of her friends from Snapchat had sent her a video. Since Lailah had hundreds of friends on Snapchat, she opted not to look at the message until she got in her car; it was probably some silly video of someone doing another dumbass challenge. She walked across the large UNCW campus until she made it to one of the student's parking lots and hopped inside her car. She turned over her ignition and moved the knob to the max on her air conditioner. Although it was the first week in May, the sun was blazing with little too few breezes going by. Lailah took out her phone and tapped on the message she ignored earlier. When she saw the people in the video, she squinted her eyes for a brief second and zoomed in closer to be sure that she was actually seeing what she was seeing. Lailah felt her chest tighten and heartbeat increase by the second as her blood began to boil with anger, tiny beads of sweat formed on her forehead, and she did everything she could do to hold back her tears. She pulled herself together then immediately sent a reply to the user whom had sent her the video.

"Bitch, I don't know if you think shit is funny, but I need you to have that same energy when I come for your ass." She fumed. She dropped her phone in her center console then quickly put her car in reverse and headed on the main highway.

"Nigga, you got me fucked up." Lailah said aloud as she gripped the steering wheel hard and bit her lip. A hundred different scenarios ran through her head as she sped towards her destination. The twenty-minute drive was cut in half and Lailah was surprised and thankful that she didn't get a ticket along the way. She parked in a parking spot that was nearest to her boyfriend's apartment and wasted no time getting out her car. Lailah walked up to the door, her short legs chopping like scissors, and opened the lock with her spare key. She then tiptoed to the bedroom and peeked her head inside as she watched him sleeping

like a baby. Lailah closed the door behind her, went to the kitchen, grabbed a big pot, and filled it with cold water. Once the water was filled up to her liking, she carefully walked back to his bedroom and opened the door. Lailah took a few steps towards the bed and threw the water on top of her boyfriend, splashing him, the walls, and the sheets.

"What the fuck!" Chris yelled, looking confused. He squirmed around in his soaked sheets until his eyes met with Lailah's. Chris got off his bed and picked up a shirt that was nearby and wiped the water from off his face and arms. "What the hell is wrong with you?! Huh?!" Chris seethed. He was ass naked as he looked at Lailah with fury in his eyes. He had never hit a woman in his life, but Lailah was definitely pushing it; his teeth were clenched together like some balled fists and he slowly fought to get ahold of himself.

"What the fuck you doing?" He demanded.

"What the fuck am I doing?" She barked. "Who the fuck do you think you playing with, Chris?"

She stood there staring at him with her arms folded across her chest and tapping her foot at the same time, her eyes had turned into slits. She was attempting to maintain her composure but everything inside of her wanted to slap the taste out of his cheating-mouth.

"What are you talking about Lailah?" He reached down then picked his boxers off the floor and quickly slipped them on, swaying slightly in the process. He'd partied until the early morning and was slightly hungover.

"Don't *what* me, mothafucka." She growled then added. "I thought you were sick." Lailah said as she opened her phone to show him the video of him getting a lap dance from a high yellow female as he gripped and slapped her ass. Towards the end of the video, him and the girl were hugged up, and he had her left nipple in his mouth and his finger was moving in and out of her vagina from the back. Then Lailah heard him say to her. *"That pussy soaking wet."*

The girl in the video moaned and started licking his neck. *"Only for a real nigga like you, daddy."* Lailah finally moved the phone down to her side and stared at him.

Then out of the blue Chris said, "That shit photoshopped, that ain't me." He couldn't think of anything else to say, but another lie came right after that one. "The same way them internet trolls be putting NBA player heads on other people bodies and stuff." He shrugged as if he'd convinced himself.

That was the icing on the cake. She let out a half ass laugh and pulled her arm back and slapped Chris so hard across his nose and face that he couldn't do anything but grab her and contain her.

"Hey calm the fuck down!" He yelled, gripping her wrist.

"Nigga you's a fucking lie!" She yelled out; she was steaming mad now and it was to the point that her lips were trembling.

What made it even worse was that the video was made just the night before. Chris had bailed out on Lailah when she'd asked him to take her to the movies and he told her that his stomach was aching and he didn't feel good. That was the only thing she could visualize right now. Then she said to him. "You don't look sick to me, Chris." Her voice was high enough to wake up the entire apartment complex. "Your dirty dick ass out here fucking around on me with some nasty ass hoe!" She screamed. "Huh?"

Chris finally took a deep drawn out breath, his eyes went to the floor and then back up to her. Trying his best to hold his composure because he had a far bigger issue on his hands besides this one. "Baby, listen. I was. . ." He began to explain. He didn't know what to say and was silently cursing out himself for being so careless.

"Shut-up! I don't wanna hear shit you got to say!" Lailah

cut him off, breaking free of his grip. She was so caught up in her emotions that she didn't notice the shower had been running from the bathroom until it went off. And in that moment, it seemed as if the world had stopped and everything was moving in slow motion. The bathroom door opened, and when Lailah's head turned towards it, she stared at the female wrapped in a towel and drying her hair. She was the same female from the video.

The girl looked shocked when she seen Lailah and Chris standing in the middle of the room. Not knowing what to do next, the girl backed up with fear in her eyes.

"You nasty lil' bitch." Lailah pointed in the girl's direction. "Bring yo trifling ass here." Lailah commanded. She had a cold look in her eyes as she stared the female up and down then said, "You think you just gonna fuck my nigga and get away with the shit?" The girl was frozen in place and was afraid to do anything in that moment.

"Look I didn't...I didn't even know he had a girl." The female stuttered.

"She lying baby," Chris chimed in.

"Shut your ass up!" Lailah snapped, slapping him again.

Chris flinched then grabbed her by the shoulders; it was an instant reflex. "I said calm the fuck down!" His voice echoed inside the room. His female guest moved to gather her clothing.

"Nigga let me go!" Lailah screamed, pulling away from him then shoving him in the chest. Her chest rose then fell with every breath as she glared at him. Chris stepped back, putting some distance between them. Lailah turned like a woman possessed then directed her attention back to the female who was hastily getting dressed.

"Where you going hoe?" Lailah questioned. The female looked at her like a child who knew they was about to get a whooping. Lailah moved in her direction.

"Baby don't. . ." Chris pleaded as he walked towards Lailah and grabbed her wrist.

Whap!

Lailah backhanded Chris so hard he stumbled back onto his bed and looked at her as if she lost her mind. Lailah was disgusted at the fact of him calling himself *protecting* his sideline hoe. When she turned her attention back to the girl, Lailah seen her trying to make a run for it but her reflexes never seemed to disappoint. Lailah grabbed the girl by her weave and slammed her roughly up against the wall. Her enemy yelped like a dog. There was blood rushing down the girl's nose, but Lailah didn't have an ounce of sympathy. She pounced on top of the girl and gave her multiple punches and slaps across her face as her victim tried her best to block the hits.

"Get off me you crazy bitch!" The female ordered, desperately attempting to dodge each lick.

"Lailah stop it!" Chris ran over and grabbed Lailah by her waist to pull her off of the girl as she tried her best to free herself from Chris's hold.

"Don't you fucking touch me! You gonna defend this bitch over me?! Fuck you!" Lailah screamed. Chris carried her out the bedroom to separate the females, but Lailah's anger was at an all-time high. Lailah shoved Chris out of her way and ran back inside the room, where she seen the girl struggling to stand up while holding on to her side. To get her point across, Lailah went up to the girl and kicked her in the stomach relentlessly before she was interrupted by Chris once again.

"Baby stop! C'mon man!" Chris pleaded. He had totally underestimated Lailah's strength because he never seen her get into a fight before. Once Lailah freed herself from Chris's grasp, she turned around and caught him off guard with a right hook that sent him to the floor. Chris' hands tightened into fist as he lay on the floor, silently reminding himself that he does not hit females. Lailah looked over at the girl who was crying a river of tears and noticed a few bruises that had appeared.

"What you crying for? You weren't crying when you were fucking my man!" She panted with anger. She waited for a response . When she didn't get one, she shook her head. "You know what...you can have him bitch." She turned then marched out the room.

"I was drunk! She don't mean shit to me! I swear!" Chris begged as he rose back up to his feet, following behind her.

"Get the fuck outta my face with that bullshit! Drunk my ass nigga! You think that gives you the greenlight to do whateva the fuck you wanna do?!" Lailah said as she swung the front door open then stepped outside.

"Lailah listen to me, I made a mistake." Chris pleaded. He was barefoot, wearing only his boxers, but he didn't care. He didn't want to lose her.

"*I* made the mistake," Lailah advised him, "Trusting your dirty ass." She felt like she was going to burst into tears; she told herself to be strong. She hit the unlock button on her keyfob then opened the driver's side door. "Why Chris?" She questioned, turning to face him. "Why?"

He stood in front of her with a look of regret and shame on his face. "I don't know--"

"You do know!" She screamed. "Tell me why!"

He looked away then took a deep breath and exhaled. "I don't know...I guess I just wanted something different."

No this mutherfucka didn't! Lailah nodded her head then laughed sadistically. "Something different? Okay." She pressed the button on her car remote and popped the trunk open. She was consumed with anger and ready to do the unthinkable. She pushed past him, went to her trunk and took out a metal baseball bat, and made her way towards Chris's Mustang.

"Lailah…" He called slowly, his eyes grew wide at the sight of the bat.

"Something different my nigga." She smiled deviously. "I got something different for your ass."

"Lailah! Stop! I'm fucking warning you!" Chris's heart started pounding; he was ready to tackle Lailah at any moment. He loved his car, which took him about three years to save up for.

"And I'm warning *you* nigga. Come any closer and I'll beat yo ass with this bat instead! Try me!" Lailah was now out for revenge and wasn't up to do anymore talking. It wasn't Chris first time cheating on her, and for all she knew, he probably fucked around many more times. Lailah twirled the bat as she walked in front of his car. "Something different." She recited then bust both his headlights. She laughed as the glass fell onto the ground. "I hope that bitch's pussy was worth every fucking minute." She roared viciously.

"I'm sorry! Now put the mothafuckin' bat down! Right now dammit!!" Chris's patience was wearing thin, even though he understood her frustration; she was taking it too far in his eyes.

"Well that's one thing you and I can agree on. You are a sorry ass motherfucker." Lailah shook her head as she walked around the car. "Sorry ass piece of shit." She laughed as she hit the glass of the passenger's side window.

"That's enough!" Chris rushed towards her. He gave her a death stare and was ready to knock her on her ass.

"Nigga, stay away from me," she yelled, swinging the bat in the air.

Chris leaned back, avoiding a hit then grabbing her wrist. "I said stop this shit!" He yelled, squeezing her wrist. The pressure he applied made Lailah wince from the pain. He pried the bat from her hands then shoved her out of anger, causing her to stumble backwards and fall.

Lailah stared up at Chris in disbelief as her anger slowly started to subside and was replaced with hurt and pain. She slowly pulled herself up off the pavement then shook her head.

"Baby…" Chris instantly felt regret for letting his anger get the best of him.

"I was a fool to think that you'd be different from the rest of these other guys out here. You turned out to be a fuck nigga just like the rest." Lailah stated sadly. She walked back towards her car, ignoring Chris's pleas. He was ultimately pissed about his car, but he wanted to desperately save his relationship with her.

"You think you just gonna fuck my shit up and leave?! At least hear me out Lailah, damn!" Chris grabbed Lailah by her shoulders and threw her against her car door. He stood in front of her huffing and puffing, attempting to calm his nerves. A few seconds had passed as he gathered his words while resisting the urge to smack Lailah silly for the damage she just caused to his car.

"I suggest you get the fuck outta my face! Hear you out for what?! So you can continue to fuckin' lie to me?! Move out my way!" Lailah gave Chris a hard shove, which resulted in him stumbling back a few feet. "We don't have shit else to talk about! You made the decision to fuck that hoe without thinking twice about my feelings! So you can take whateva excuse you have and shove it up yo ass! It's *over* between us." Lailah replied firmly.

"Baby, don't do this to us. You're gonna throw away three years for that bitch? Who I don't give a fuck about? Her pussy was whack anyways. She ain't got shit on you baby. Don't do this Lai. I love you too much to just let you go." Chris said as he stood back in front of Lailah, stroking her cheek while looking into her eyes. Chris hoped and prayed his usual manipulation would get him out of the situation at hand but unfortunately, his luck ran out this time around.

"Bye Chris." Lailah opened her car door and hopped inside. She turned over the ignition and almost ran Chris over when she backed out of her spot. Lailah sped off with tears streaming down her face as she drove. She felt like she was the blame for the pain she was experiencing now. Lailah thought had she not given their relationship one more shot, she would've saved herself the heartache. She hated that she loved Chris but love was no longer enough; it was clear he had no respect for her. Lailah drove in silence for fifteen minutes until she reached her destination. She turned into the Reserve Mayfaire apartment complex and parked into an available spot. She turned off her ignition as she took in a few deep breaths. Lailah didn't know what her next move was gonna be, so she turned to her best friend for some much needed guidance. Lailah stepped out her car and walked up one flight of steps until she got to the front door.

Knock! Knock! Knock!

"It's about time you got here. I was about. . ." Janae stopped midsentence when she saw Lailah's red puffy eyes. She quickly pulled her inside then said, "Tell me what's going on." Janae led Lailah to the living room and sat down beside her on the couch, handing her a box of tissues.

"Chris. . ." Lailah managed to get out and started bawling once more. Anytime she opened her mouth to speak, she felt like she would choke on her words. She felt weak and hopeless that Chris's actions had so much control over her. Lailah felled into Janae's arms and cried like a baby until she had no more tears to cry.

"What that nigga do? Don't tell me he put his hands on you." Janae guessed and looked over at her friend who shook her head no. Janae watched Lailah take out her iPhone and showed her the video that answered her question. "No this nigga didn't!" Janae spat. Her heart went out to her friend in that moment because she knew how deep Lailah's love went for Chris. "Look, that nigga ain't worth you stressing over him. He ain't shit and never was. Hell, if anything, you gave that nigga life." She shook her head. Lailah had given Janae the entire scoop of what went down at Chris's place.

"Damn, you wasn't playing no games. That nigga betta consider himself lucky cause if I were you, I woulda did more damage than that." Janae commented. Lailah laughed lightly. Janae was glad she could put a smile on her best friend's face in the midst of her feeling down.

"I'm glad this shit didn't pop off in the middle of the semester. I don't need any drama coming in between me and my schooling." Lailah stated. With straight A's in tow, Lailah was determined to finish out her junior year strong.

"I feel you on that. You shoulda let me handle them for you so your school career wouldn't end up in jeopardy. Cause ol' girl might press charges on yo ass." Janae chuckled. She opened a pack of The Game silver and took out both cigars and placed them on her rolling tray. "The plug just left before you came." Janae added. She took out two nuggets that sat in a clear jar and placed them in her grinder.

"Good. And nah, I can't afford you going to jail either. You'd wipe my savings account out fo sho." Lailah laughed but was serious at the same time. She chuckled and wiped away a few more tears that had escaped. Lailah and Janae had been best friends since the seventh grade; they were closer than sisters and more loyal than lovers.

"My parents would take care of it." Janae said as she admired the neatness of her two blunts. She gave one to Lailah and a lighter as well. They both lit up the loud and took a few drags before continuing their conversation.

"Yea, you right. Have you took up their offer or you still deciding?"

"I accepted, but I don't know where I wanna go yet. I ain't trynna stay here in punk-ass Wilmington any longer." Janae ranted. Both her parents had made the mistake and spoiled her rotten with their money. Janae's father owned a construction company while her mother ran a catering business that specialized in soul food and desserts. Janae's parents grew tired of Janae's bratty ways, so they gave her an ultimatum of getting a degree or they would cut off her financial sources completely. "I mean, isn't my degree from Cape Fear good enough? Hell, that alone was gruesome."

"Your parents just want you to further your education and not settle for less. I mean think about it, what kind of job that pays well would accept your associates in arts? Hmm? I'm just saying. Shit people with bachelor's degrees are barely getting anywhere, let alone getting paid the amount they deserve. Which is why I have no other choice but getting my Master's. It was my plan from the beginning anyway." Lailah explained. The effects from the loud had her feeling right and relaxed. The events that occurred earlier were now pushed to the back of her mind.

"I see. I was thinking about attending either A&T or Central." Janae picked up the remote to her 40" inch plasma TV that was mounted on the wall in front of them. She skimmed through the channels and was disappointed when she couldn't find anything worth watching. Janae got up and placed *Set It Off* in her DVD player.

"So you leaving this fall?"

"Hell no. I'ma wait a year before going." Janae flopped back on the sofa and finished what was left of her blunt. Being a true smoker, she rolled up another two blunts to fulfill her needs.

"A year? Why so long?" Lailah needed to understand

Janae's reasoning because unlike her, Lailah had bills and student debt to worry about. Janae was blessed to have parents that could pay for her education easily but was too blind to see it.

"To be honest, I'm a little nervous about moving to another city. Wilmington is all I know. I just want to be established first before going off."

"I understand. Well, your timing couldn't have been more perfect. Since I only have one more year, I have no problem going to graduate school at a different institution. I always wanted to attend an HBCU. I just have to see if they offer my degree in their graduate program."

"Sounds good to me. I'll let you know when I make my final decision. But not to destroy the mood, but are you done with Chris? For real for real?" Janae wanted to see where Lailah's head was because she was good for always going back to Chris. Janae felt like her friend could find way better, seeing at how pretty and intelligent Lailah was.

"Fuck that nigga. The dick was getting sloppy anyway. I'm done dating until I know for sure it's real. I'm over wasting my time on these clown ass niggas." Lailah ranted.

"Well shit if that's the case, what made you stay as long as you did?"

"I'm not one to just give up on someone I truly love. I honestly thought he had changed but obviously not." Lailah rolled her eyes. She was done sulking over Chris and made a promise to only focus on her studies and nothing else.

"I see you redecorated again." Lailah stated, changing the subject as she looked around at the décor of Janae's living room. Janae had expensive taste, which was expressed in her two-bedroom luxury apartment. It had dark hardwood floors in every room, granite counter tops with an all-white kitchen, a private balcony, and stainless-steel appliances. Janae had a light grey sectional sofa with white and silver decorative pillows to match, and a huge white fuzzy rug that was positioned under her dark grey coffee table. Along with a nice place to call home, Janae drove a silver 2019 BMW 230i. Ever since she'd been in the world, Janae had never went without and her parents made sure to supply her with nothing but the best.

"Yes, girl. It was past time. I needed something different. You hungry? Now you know my ass ain't gonna cook. You cool with ordering Dominos?" Janae asked as she grabbed her phone that laid beside her.

"That's fine. Wat'chu got sweet in there to eat?" Lailah ate nothing but sweets to cover up her depression. Although she was done with Chris, it would take a while for her to get over the feelings she had for him; letting love go was never easy.

"There's some brownie mix in there, ice cream, and chocolate covered pretzels. Help yourself." Janae offered. She decided not to bring up Chris any more in their conversation and would help her friend get over him in any way possible.

CHAPTER 2

"Shitttt!!" Zion moaned as he shot a huge load down Toree's throat. He gripped a handful of her hair while biting his lip. "Stop. Stop." Zion said as Toree continued to suck on his dick. He was already feeling like he was on top of a mountain from the explosive orgasm he just had. He looked down at Toree, who was giggling at his response, and shook his head. Zion took a few more minutes to recuperate before finally getting up to take a shower. As usual, Toree's good pussy and dangerous head game had him spent and he was ready to start his day.

"I'm gonna go make something to eat." Toree winked. She slipped on the black see through teddy that she had worn the night before while waiting for Zion's response. When he didn't reply, she walked out the bedroom and headed out to her kitchen.

"I bet you are." Zion said to himself. He went into her bathroom and closed the door behind him, so he could be alone with his thoughts. He knew Toree had something up her sleeve and wasn't in the mood to stick around for it. While in

the shower, Zion decided to kill two birds with one stone and washed his fro because it had been well overdue. Forty minutes later, he was fully dressed, wearing a striped mint green and white shirt that brought out his chocolate skintone, tan shorts, and white Air Force Ones. His president gold Rolex gave his outfit the final touch. His stomach started grumbling like crazy once the aroma of bacon floated from the kitchen, dancing around his nostrils. His original instinct had told him to get out as quickly as possible, but he figured he'd take advantage of the situation, so he could avoid stopping anywhere to grab something to eat. Zion walked over to the nightstand, grabbed his keys and his phone, and then stuck them in his pockets. He then walked out to the kitchen and took a seat at the bar, where Toree had a plate waiting for him. She had made grits, eggs, bacon, and biscuits, which was Zion's favorite meal for breakfast.

"So, what's your plans for today?" Zion broke the silence between them as he took some margarine and placed it in his grits. He enjoyed the view from looking at Toree's fat ass, which had a huge tattoo of a butterfly that covered the majority of her cheeks.

"Eh, most likely go shopping with the girls. I haven't seen them in a while." Toree poured Zion and herself a glass of orange juice. She instantly caught the smirk that was on his face and confronted him on it. "What's so funny?" Her voice dripped with a slight attitude as she placed one hand on her hip.

"What? I can't smile?" Zion said in a sarcastic tone. He shook his head and continued to eat his food. He was getting closer to the truth behind Toree's fake act.

"You can but don't try to act like it wasn't a reason behind it." Toree sucked her teeth. She walked back over to the stove and began making loud noises by moving pots and pans into the sink.

"If you say so. Have you thought about getting a job to occupy your time?" Zion knew he was pressing all the right buttons and was low-key enjoying every minute of it.

"For what? As long as my bills get paid, ion give a fuck. So why should I? You ain't never had a problem with me working, so what's the issue all of a sudden?" Toree snapped her head back in Zion's direction. She was offended and pissed by the way Zion was coming at her.

"Why you getting mad? It was just a question." Zion asked. He wanted to quickly finish his meal before his conversation with Toree led him to losing his appetite. "All I'm saying is, you need to stop relying on me and other niggas to keep giving yo ass handouts and shit. You've gotten too damn comfortable for me and it's unattractive." Zion took out his phone and started scrolling through social media.

"What you mean *other niggas*? You know good and fucking well you're the only one who gives me money!" Toree lied. She tried her best to put on her poker face, but the way Zion kept throwing shots at her only made her look more guilty. Zion quickly shot her a look that read she was full of shit.

"Bitch you must think I'm stupid. You wanna insult my intelligence and shit." Zion got up and proceeded to leave but was immediately stopped when Toree stepped in front of the door.

"Zion, wait! Don't leave. Yes, other dudes pay my bills, but they don't matter to me! You know my heart is yours and that you're the only one I love." Toree couldn't help herself and felt now was the time to express her true feelings, once again. They had been dealing with each other for almost four years. Even though Zion had told Toree not to catch feelings from the very beginning and Toree agreed. Somewhere down the road, she had broken the rules and made the mistake of getting caught up with a dude who wasn't into cuffing anyone. "I know you feel something for me. You can't stand there and say that you don't." Toree said as she pressed both of her hands against Zion's chest. He gave her the look of disgust in return and moved her hands away.

"I don't. I meant what I had said and it's obvious you didn't listen. I made shit crystal clear between us but yo ass wanted more. And you know I can't give you that." Zion laughed on the inside because he got to the bottom of why Toree was being so extra with being nice and making breakfast. He couldn't see himself being with a woman like Toree for many reasons. She was selfish, unambitious, and a liar. In order for Zion to even consider a commitment with a female, she had to have some basic attributes that Toree couldn't even comprehend.

"I can't believe you. You wanna play with my heart as if I ain't shit!" Toree now had tears streaming down her face.

"Cut the bullshit. You knew from the jump we were never gonna be together, and I didn't give you that impression either. So stop being so fucking dramatic." Zion said.

Toree was a pretty girl who stood at 5'1, meaty thighs, light skin with jet-black silky hair that stopped at her shoulders. The fact that she didn't set any goals for herself or had got too accustomed to her fast lifestyle was a major turn-off for Zion. The only reason Zion kept fucking with Toree was because she had good pussy and a killer head game; other than that, she had nothing else going for herself. Zion wanted to be tied to a woman one day, but she had to be extra special for him to give up his ways to settle down.

"Well fuck you then Zion! Lose my fuckin' number and get the fuck out!" Toree yelled as she moved to the side. She took the risk and put her heart on the line only for Zion to rip it to shreds with his harsh comments. She hated herself for listening to her heart instead of her mind.

"No problem. But you might wanna reconsider about getting a job or some sort of income cause this will be the *last* time you'll receive anything from me." Zion smiled as he went into his pocket and threw a wad of one hundred-dollar bills against Toree's chest that fell to the floor. "That should cover your next month's rent and car payment." Zion replied, looking at a crying Toree. He walked out the door while slamming it behind him.

Zion got inside his white Chevy Camaro and headed onto highway 17. He was glad to be done with Toree and felt like a huge weight had been lifted off his shoulders. He turned onto a long dirt road until he reached a small house that looked abandoned. Zion parked his car in front of the home then turned off the engine. His phone had buzzed a few times in the cup holder where it was placed. He looked at the five missed texts from Toree and dismissed every one of them. He scrolled on his phone and went to her contact information and blocked her. Zion got out his car and made his way inside the house. One of his best friends Derell was sitting at the table in the kitchen, focused on counting the stacks of cash in front of him. Zion went over and gave him a quick pound and sat down in a chair beside him.

"Wassup brah? What's it looking like?" Zion got straight to the point. He was a man who was about his business and not one to beat around the bush when it came to his money.

"Everything's here except we have a small issue." Derell informed. Knowing Zion's short temper, he had to tread carefully on what he was about to tell him.

"I'm listening." Zion gave Derell a serious look and sat back in his chair.

"Lil man came up short again. I don't know what's his problem, but this is the second time." Derell explained. He looked over at Zion, who didn't show any emotion whatsoever and couldn't tell what he was thinking. There was a brief moment of silence before Zion spoke again.

"Mmm. Tell him to bring his ass here." Zion finally answered. Zion watched Derell nod his head as he stopped what he was a doing and placed a call.

"He said he's on the way." Derell confirmed as he hung up his phone. "What's going on with you?" Derell could tell something was bothering Zion as soon as he walked in the door but finally chose to address it. They had been friends since elementary school and their friendship had been tested many times, but nothing could break the bond they shared.

"Toree. I had to cut that bitch off. She right steady trynna force something that ain't meant to be." Zion vented. His expression was a clear indication that he was frustrated.

"Mmm. I been told you to stop fucking with her, but you ain't wanna listen to me. You wanna learn the hard way and shit. But we'll see how long this will last." Derell didn't believe Zion when it came to Toree because he said the same thing many times before. Zion would cut her off then give it a week or two and he'd be right back to fucking her. Derell wasn't a fan of Toree . He couldn't stand a female that used niggas for money.

"Well I'm serious this time. I was getting bored with her pussy anyway, plus I know I'm not the only one she be fucking. But what pisses me off the most is she wanna play me like a fool or sum shit." He grunted. "So before I left, I gave her the last allowance she'll ever get from me."

"Allowance?" Derell stared at him with raised eyebrows. "I wouldn't have gave her ass shit. Bitch would have been lucky to get the dick." He shook his head then exhaled. "You's a good one. She wouldn't have got a penny outta me." Derell stated as he wrapped a rubber band around the stack of money he just finished counting.

"I know. Cause you a mean mothafucka." Zion laughed.

"Shit, at least you know." Derell agreed. "Allowance.." He repeated. "That's what's wrong with these hoes now. Niggas like you got them feeling special because they giving up the pussy or got some decent ass head." He snorted then continued, "These hoes don't deserve no reward or *allowance* for letting a nigga fuck. Hell, their asses wanna fuck too. In fact," he snapped his fingers, "send that bitch an invoice. She should be paying you for the dick." They both laughed.

"Nigga you stupid." Zion chuckled.

Derell smiled. He was serious but happy that he could make his partner smile. Derell only wanted to see Zion happy and for him to have the best that life had to offer.

"So what you doing for your birthday?" Derell questioned, deciding it was time to change the subject.

"I haven't decided yet. I just know I don't want no fuckin' party, that's for sure." Zion was turning twenty-six and wanted more than just to party and turn up. He had plans to go overseas but had no one to share his time with. It was moments like these where he wished he had that special someone in his life.

"I was thinking maybe go to the islands and shit. Go mingle with some foreign beauties and party with them." Derell suggested. He looked over at Zion, who was pondering his idea as he placed the last stack of cash in its pile which came to a million dollars.

"I'll think about it." Zion replied. "Look tell that lil nigga to meet us at the main spot instead. And tell Shawn to come as well." He instructed.

"Aight." Derell had a devious smile across his face. He knew what Zion was up to and was ready to take a front row seat. Derell got up and carefully placed each stack of money in the hidden vault that was under the floorboards in the bedroom. He then followed Zion out the house, locking the door behind them.

They both got in their cars and drove to their destination, the Brunswick Forest Plantation, which was a private home development.

CHAPTER 3

Zion pulled his car into the two-car garage with Derell parking next to him. They hopped out of their vehicles and hurried inside the customized home. Zion's main stash house was a modern two-story house that had four bedrooms, three and a half baths with a finished sound proof basement. Once Zion walked towards the living room, he acknowledged a few of his workers; Joe, Kel, X, and Zay led them downstairs to the basement where Shawn and Jalen were waiting.

"Good evening fellas." Zion greeted both Shawn and Jalen. He smirked when he noticed the expression of worry on their faces was almost synonymous.

"Good evening." Shawn and Jalen said in unison.

Zion went over to the bar that was in the corner of the room and fixed himself a shot of Hennessey. After he took the shot to the head, he motioned for Shawn and Jalen to stand up while he took a seat behind the small desk in the room. Zion looked at both the boys with intensity, taking a brief pause before continuing.

"So, Shawn. You got my money or you still fucking

around?" Zion questioned. He looked at Shawn, who had sweat forming on his forehead and was continuously making sniffling sounds. He was disappointed in Shawn more than anything because he knew his background. Zion knew that Shawn was getting high off the supply he gave him because the signs had been there. Zion had a lot of anger built up and felt betrayed by Shawn.

"I'ma get it. I swear… I just need a lil more time, I got this brah. Trust me." Shawn said. He was close to shitting in his pants and prayed that Zion would have mercy on him once again. He owed Zion a total of five bands and now, he was on the verge of paying with his life.

"I gave you more than enough time and yet, you still came up empty-handed. The only thing you been doing was trynna find yo next fix. And your work and services have become redundant at this point. You turned into a fucking junkie nigga, and that shit don't fly with me." Zion watched Shawn put his head down in shame. "I ran into yo baby mama Joy the other day, and she was pissed because you stole money out her purse that was supposed to go towards y'all's rent. You went as low as stealing from yo family? Like nigga what the fuck?" Zion was disgusted with Shawn's actions; they reminded him of what he had endured during his childhood. He was the product of a broken-fatherless home and a heroin- addicted mother, who had often put her addiction before the needs of her child. Zion's mother would sell the shoes off his feet for her next fix; she'd proven this more than once. Despite the way he hated how addiction affected families and made children suffer, Zion stepped into the drug game when he was fourteen. In some small way, he felt if he became the dealer, he was taking back what life had taken from him. It was a twisted thought but Zion held it as his truth.

"You're no good to me anymore. And quite frankly our

business is done." He continued to speak to Shawn as he stood, pulling his weapon from underneath his shirt.

"Zion, man… come on," Shawn begged with his hands up. "I'll get the money man! Come on Zion, I…I got a family." He continued to plead, hoping that Zion would have mercy upon him.

"You got a family?" Zion replied staring him in the eyes. "You do don't you?" His question was a rhetorical one. "A family that you're stealing from and fucking over for your own selfish desires. A family that I know is going to be better off without you."

Pop! Pop! Pop!

Shawn's murder happened so quickly that Jalen hadn't had time to blink. It was his first time seeing someone get shot and he felt like he was about to piss his pants. His heart raced as chills crept down his spine. A single tear trickled down his cheek as he tried to mentally prepare to meet his maker. He looked down at Shawn's lifeless body, staring into his open eyes. They were wide as saucers. Zion tucked his Glock 45 back into his waistband then sat back down in his chair. His attitude was calm as ever as he looked at Jalen, whose breathing became more and more intense with every second.

"Now Jalen. It's come to my attention that you're short two bands." Zion spoke calmly.

"I…I…ran into some issues with some niggas I thought I could trust." Jalen responded honestly.

"You thought? You can't *think* when you're dealing with other people's shit Jalen. You better *know*. Understood?"

"Yes…" Jalen answered nervously.

"Good. Now my advice to you is to take heed to my first and *only* warning. If you don't wanna end up like Shawn, I suggest you get the rest of my money. You have three days." Zion said seriously.

Zion had been in Jalen's shoes when he first started deal-ing, which is why he decided to give him one more chance. Jalen was nineteen years old and had shown a lot of potential that helped seal his position with Zion. He could be great in the game; but first, he had to learn to be careful with whom he trusted with the product and to never be short with another man's money.

Kel and X grabbed Jalen and escorted him upstairs and out the home while Joe and Zay got rid of Shawn's body then started the process of cleaning the area of evidence.

"Damn, you surprised my ass." Derell stated as he walked towards Zion. He didn't know Zion's true reason for letting Jalen live but didn't feel the need to question him either.

"I was nineteen once. So I completely understand. I'm pretty sure it's his nerves and he's overwhelmed now that he knows being in this business isn't as easy as he thought. But that doesn't mean he's excluded from the rules. Just hope he can get his shit together in time." Zion liked Jalen and his personality but would have to charge his death to the game if he didn't follow through. "And I made up my mind about my birthday. I'ma just get drunk and chill." Zion informed him as he walked upstairs with Derell following close behind.

"What? Why? Man, yo ass is getting boring." Derell stated. He followed Zion into the kitchen, taking a seat on one of the cushioned stools at the kitchen island. He was slightly surprised that Zion was opting to just get fucked up for his birthday, but at the same time, he had a feeling his friend wouldn't be up for anything. Lately, besides fucking Toree, Zion would make trips to Florida to meet with their connect and spent the majority of his time at home.

"Because I don't feel like doing shit. That's why. I'm content with just relaxing for a change. Plus I ain't missing out on nothing anyways. If I change my mind, I'll let you know. But I doubt I will." Zion looked into his fridge and took out a pack of New York strip steaks, placed them on the counter, and grabbed a couple beers, handing one to Derell.

"Thanks brah." Derell stated, twisting the top of his bottle.

Zion removed a large George Foreman from underneath the cabinet then set it on the counter. He set the temperature to his preference then started preparing the steaks to be cooked.

"You must've heard my stomach." Derell chuckled before taking a long swig of his beer.

"Shit, that and I was getting hungry my damn self." Zion laughed as he seasoned their steaks. Twenty minutes later, Zion placed their food on the kitchen table. He'd prepared a small feast consisting of steaks, loaded baked potatoes, salad, and breadsticks. The two of them made brotherly conversation and several laughs throughout their meal. After they finished eating dinner, Zion did a final check in the basement to make sure everything was perfect before doing a quick inventory of his product that was hidden in one of the bedrooms. When he made certain that nothing was missing, he met Derell in the garage and said his goodbyes. Zion got in his car, cranked up his stereo, and played Flipp Dinero's *Leave Me Alone* as he drove back to Wilmington.

Before going home Zion made a quick stop by Wal-Mart. He'd been so busy with business, he'd forgotten he was almost out of one of his important personal item. He walked inside the store and went straight for the aisle that contained the deodorant.

"You gotta be shitting me." Zion said to himself. He looked at the empty slot that took place of the only deodorant he used and looked to see no extras on the top shelf. Frustrated, he left out the aisle and seen an associate who was stocking the shelves with toothpaste.

"Excuse me." Zion asked, trying to get the female's attention.

"Yes, can I help you with something?" The woman asked as she turned to face Zion.

"Damn." Zion mumbled, admiring her features.

She smiled, causing him to be temporarily rendered speechless. After a few seconds, he finally regained his composure and said, "I'm sorry. Uh... I was wondering when you guys would get more of the Degree cool comfort back in." Zion wondered who the gorgeous woman was standing before him. She rocked her natural hair in a big puff as her baby hairs were slicked to perfection. He couldn't tell if she was wearing contacts or her eye color was all natural but her light-brown eyes had him slightly hypnotized. She had smooth brown skin and stood at 5'3. Her uniform did no justice when it came to her petite frame and thick thighs. The fact that she captured his attention in her work uniform spoke high volumes to Zion. There was something about her that drew him to her besides her natural beauty, and he longed to discover what that something was.

"We have a truck coming tonight, so we should have some by tomorrow." The woman answered.

"Thank you. I didn't catch ya name." Zion stated while noticing she wasn't wearing a name badge.

"Lailah." She answered softly.

"Lailah." He replied then smiled. "I like that."

CHAPTER 4

*J*t had been two weeks since Lailah had taken her last exam and she was on her laptop reading her final grades. Seeing all A's and her GPA being at a 3.9, she was slightly irritated because she was aiming for a 4.0. Now that her summer had officially started, her main objective was to work as much overtime as possible before the fall semester came back around. Lailah got up from her bed and took a long hot shower. After feeling refreshed, she went into her closet and put on a yellow strapless romper and tan *rainbow* flip-flops. She gelled her hair into a high bun and ran a layer of soft pink lip-gloss across her full lips. The chiming of her cellphone indicated she had received a new text message. She walked over to the nightstand then picked up her phone.

Nae Bug: Hey girly, I'm outside. C'mon my ass is hungry. Lol.

Lailah smiled at Janae's text as she removed her keys and purse from the closet doorknob and headed out the door.

* * *

"Wassup?" Lailah greeted her once she hopped inside the car.

"Not shit. So how'd you do on your final grades?" Janae asked as she backed her car out of the parking space and headed onto the main street. She was taking Lailah out to eat to one of her favorite seafood restaurants.

"All A's and I was one point away from getting my four-point-o." Lailah explained. "Now that really pissed me off." She confessed.

"Mm, I see. Well I'm pretty sure *Mae's Seafood* will help you get over that one point." Janae winked.

"Oh, so that's where we're going?" Lailah pretended like she wasn't excited but deep down was happier than ever.

"Oh, please. Don't try to act like you ain't ready for them fantails bitch." Janae and Lailah busted out in laughter. Janae could tell her friend was putting up a huge front and that there was something else on her mind.

"Yeah, my greedy ass is more than ready. And for them hushpuppies as well." Lailah said, licking her bottom lip.

Once they finally reached the famous establishment, Lailah pointed out an empty parking space to her friend.

"I hope there's a free spot in our favorite section." Janae commented as they headed inside.

Janae asked the hostess if there was a table available on the third floor and luckily there was. Their hostess led them to their table and gave them each their menus.

"This view will never get old." Lailah said in awe. Being on the top floor, they had a nice ocean view because the restaurant sat on top of the water. The deck was very spacious and there was plenty of shade from the carefully planted trees for people who chose to eat outside.

"Good afternoon, my name is Kayla and I'll be your server. Could I start you off with something to drink?" Their waitress was a Caucasian female, who looked to be no more than eighteen. She had brunette curly hair and freckles that decorated her face.

"Um, I'm gonna have an ice water with lemon." Lailah answered.

"I'll have the same." Janae replied. "Also, could you bring us some extra lemons?"

"Yes ma'am." Kayla said as she left to go fill their drink orders.

"Soooo what are you getting?" Lailah asked. Her mind was already made up on her entrée.

"I'ma try sum different. I need to expand." Janae looked over her menu intensely.

A few minutes passed and their waitress returned. "Have you ladies decided or do you need a few more minutes?" Kayla asked. She carefully sat both of their drinks on the table and a small bowl of lemon slices per Janae's request.

"Nah, we're ready. I'm gonna have the fantail shrimp dinner with coleslaw and a baked potato with extra sour cream please and an order of hushpuppies. And that'll do me, hun." Lailah said as she handed her menu to Kayla.

"Alrighty, and for you?" Kayla questioned, looking in Janae's direction.

"I'm gonna go with the seafood platter with extra shrimp, coleslaw and French fries for my sides." Janae gave up her menu as well. She watched their waitress take off to go put in their orders.

"So, have you spoken to Chris lately?" Janae was curious and hoped her best friend didn't give in like she always did.

"Hell nah. That nigga is blocked. He kept calling me like a hundred times. I guess he finally realized that he really fucked up this time and that I'm not coming back." Lailah still felt somewhat vulnerable after finding out about Chris' infidelity and just wanted to heal in peace.

"Good. You coulda did way better than him anyways. I'm

just relieved you're finally moving on cause honestly his trifling ass didn't deserve a second chance. Real shit."

"Yea, I know. But any who. Have you made a decision yet?" Lailah wanted to change the subject before she got emotional.

"No and my folks are getting impatient."

"Shit, me too. What are you waiting for? Nae, a lot of people would kill to have the opportunities and resources you have. And the fact that you're just winging this shit is ridiculous." Lailah got frustrated at how ungrateful Janae would act at times.

"I know, I know. My parents preach to me enough... I don't need you tagging along with them." Janae got defensive but knew Lailah was right.

"And that's what's wrong wit'cha ass, you don't wanna listen to nobody. All we're trynna do is teach you about the way the world works. Everything in life is NOT gonna be handed to you and that your gonna have to work for it. Your main problem is, no offense by the way, is that your parents made the mistake and created a monster. You expect every-thing to be given to you and it's sad to say and watch. I love you but that's honestly how you are." Lailah ranted. She saw the soft expression on Janae's face and reached over and held her hand.

"You're right but it ain't my fault. I'm trying to do things on my own, but it's not gonna happen overnight." Janae lowered her head and wiped away a tear from her eye. She hated feeling like everyone was coming down on her. She was trying to find her own path, but it seemed like she wasn't moving fast enough.

"I know. I just want the best for you is all. I don't wanna see you get hurt out here cause it's a cruel ass world we live in. I can tell ya that." Lailah got excited when she seen their food being brought their way.

"Greedy behind." Janae chuckled, catching on to Lailah's mood change.

"Do you ladies need anything else?" Kayla asked as she set their food and a short stack of napkins on their table.

"I believe we're good. Thank you." Janae stated as she watched the young girl leave to check on her other customers.

"Soooooo, in other news... I met this dude a couple weeks back." Lailah smiled from ear to ear.

"Oh, shittt. Where?" Janae looked excited as she ate a piece of fish from her plate.

"At work. He was looking for some type of Degree deodorant and asked when we'd be getting in more. He was fine as fuck!" Lailah expressed. The mystery guy secured a spot in her mind, and she hoped they would run into each other again.

"Details bitch. I'm all ears."

"Well he's chocolate, tall, athletic, can dress his ass off, which is always a plus. He has a fro and his curls are popping, oh my Godddddd!! And both his arms are covered in tattoos." Lailah squealed.

"Okay, okay. Sounds nice. What's his name?"

"I don't know." Lailah said disappointed.

"The fuck? You got everything but his name? Did you at least get his number?" Janae sucked her teeth as Lailah shook her head no. "I am highly upset wit'chu. I taught yo ass betta than that." Janae ran her manicured fingers down her face in frustration. "You'll prolly see him again, and when you do, don't mess up."

"I'm not worried about him. My focus is on my studies. I ain't trynna get into another relationship just to be let down again." Lailah was only being halfway serious. On one hand, she needed time to get over her ex Chris, and on the other hand, she was curious to know who the secretive guy was.

"I hear you. I just want you to have fun and do what's best for you and your heart." Janae advised her. The two of them continued to consume their meals in silence.

"So what's up wit'chu and ol' boy? I haven't heard you talk about him in a while." Lailah asked as she took a bite from one of her shrimp.

"Who? Rod?" Janae rolled her eyes. She took a sip from her water before continuing.

"Yep. Mr. Rodrick," Lailah laughed.

"I been cut that nigga off."

"Awe. What happened?"

"Ain't no damn 'awe.' He was too boring for me. I'm tired of being the one to bring life to a conversation. That shit gets old after a while. My significant other has to be as interesting as I am. Point blank period." Janae spat.

"I definitely feel you on that." Lailah nodded her head in agreement. She sat back and rubbed her small belly, feeling full.

"Plus his dick was small anyways." Janae added.

"Y'all fucked?"

"Almost until he whipped it out." She frowned with disgust. "I don't know what he thought he was finna do with that mini Vienna, but I couldn't do shit with it." Janae flagged down their waitress and asked for to-go boxes. When their waitress returned, she informed them that their bill had been paid.

"Are you sure there isn't a mistake?" Janae questioned. She looked over at Lailah who had the same confused look on her face.

"I'm positive." The waitress left declining Janae's tip as well. "What the hell? You know anybody that works here?" She looked around, attempting to spot the responsible party.

"Nah. You?" Lailah looked at Janae who shook her head.

"Well it was very nice of them, whoever it was. I guess we'll find out eventually."

"True but it better not be some bullshit because they chose to pay it forward." Janae stated bluntly.

CHAPTER 5

*J*t was still early and Lailah had a few hours to
spare, so she decided to pay her mother a visit.
Lailah hadn't seen her mother since her spring break, which
was back in March. She made the forty-minute drive to
Calabash and entered the Spring Mill , parking behind her
mother's Nissan Maxima. As soon as she stepped out of her
vehicle, she felt the familiar sting of a mosquito on the back
of her arm. "*Shit,*" she blurted, knowing not to but unable to
resist the urge to scratch. Being raised in the country had its
pros and cons. Lailah was glad to have access to the beach
anytime she wanted but hated the annoyance of mosquitoes
and insects that came along with it. She walked up to the
front door then ringed the doorbell. Seconds later, her
mother Natalie welcomed her with open arms.

"Lailah, it's good to see you."

"Hey mama."

"Come in...come in." Natalie stepped back, allowing her
room to enter. "So how's things been going on your end?"
She asked as she led Lailah to the dining room.

"They're going okay. I finished out the semester will all

A's and work has been the same." Lailah stated. "What about you?"

"Well Lauren haven't been by to check on Heaven in almost three weeks. She's been running behind this boy that's eight years older than her. She is such an embarrassment."

"Are you serious? When I see her, that's gone be her ass! You can believe that." Lailah was beyond pissed when she heard the news about her younger sister. She was so angry that she didn't realize she had slipped up and cussed in front of her mother, which is something she never did. "Sorry ma, but she needs to be held accountable for her actions. She can't just leave her child here for you to raise while she goes out and does whatever she pleases." Lailah fumed.

"I couldn't agree with you more. But I don't want you two fighting. You can tell your sister how you feel without having to put your hands on her." Natalie was one who didn't condone violence but knew she was wasting her breath because once Lailah had her mind made up, there was no talking her out of it.

"No disrespect ma... but I really ain't trynna hear that. Some people need a beatdown in order for your point to get across, and Lauren is one of those people." It was hard for Lailah to respect her mother's wishes, seeing as how her and her sister never saw eye to eye. "If daddy was here, she wouldn't be doing that crap." This was a perfect moment when Lailah wished her father was still living. Her father Anthony, who was a retired Sergeant in the Navy, had died from a hit and run accident on his way home one evening. Lailah had a close relationship with her father, which made his passing hard to accept.

"She sure wouldn't. I feel like that's the reason why she been acting out. She misses him just as much as we do."

Natalie's husband had been the voice of reason in their household and was the rock of their family.

"Maybe so but that doesn't excuse her reckless behavior ma. You babied her way too much growing up, which is one of her problems now." Lailah spat. She didn't feel bad for calling her mother out because she had been a pushover towards Lauren for years.

"Where is this coming from?" Natalie was shocked at Lailah's statement, and it showed on her face. "What's the matter with you? I never babied Lauren or you."

"Forget it ma. Where's Heaven? Sleep?"

Arguing with her mother was the last thing Lailah wanted to do. She quickly changed the subject before the situation got out of hand. Lailah and her sister were each of their parents' favorite, which was one of the reasons why they never got along. However, Lailah was happy to extend an olive branch when Lauren wasn't on some dumb shit and right now, leaving her daughter for three weeks without making contact was some dumb shit. Lailah couldn't wait until she saw her sister, so she could get off in her ass.

* * *

"OKAYYYY, I SEE YOU!" Janae hyped, looking over Lailah's outfit. They were in Janae's living room pregaming before heading out to the club. Janae handed the half of blunt to Lailah, who was looking at herself in the mirror on the wall picking at her curls.

"Thank you. You looking mighty fine ya self." Lailah commented. She was high as a kite and was ready to have some much needed fun. Work and school had been taking up the majority of her time, and she was beyond ready to let loose and unwind. Lailah wore an all-white two-piece matching set. Her halter top exposed her c-cup breasts as her high-waisted shorts hugged at her small waist. The butterfly belly ring she chose showcased her flat stomach.

"You 'bout ready?" Janae asked as she grabbed her car keys off the counter. It had been a hot minute since she went out with her friend because Lailah was more of a homebody; Janae was determined that tonight was going to be lit.

"Yep. Let's go." Lailah confirmed.

She followed behind Janae, making sure to lock the door behind them. She hopped in the passenger's seat and relaxed against Janae's leather interior. Lailah connected her Bluetooth from her phone and turned up the volume as she played Young Scooter's *Jugg King.* Lailah and Janae bopped their heads to the music as they made the fifteen-minute drive to Club Dres.

When they arrived at their destination, Janae became anxious looking at the parking lot.

"It's packed out this mothafucka. Damn!" Janae stated as she searched for a space to park. It was as if luck was on their side when there was a free space that was close to the entrance. Janae backed her car in and turned off the engine. She looked in her personal mirror to do a double check on her make-up. Janae was equally as beautiful as her best friend. She was Black and Dominican and wore her natural hair into a tapered short haircut with a side bang. She stood at 5'6 and had colorful tattoos covering her back. The dark tan spaghetti dress she wore hugged at her curvy figure. They took a few minutes to get their selves together then exited the vehicle.

"Let's see what the hype is about. I been waiting to come here for the longest." Janae said as they walked towards the front entrance.

"What took you so long?" Lailah wondered as they approached the bouncer.

After showing their IDs to the bouncer, they made their

way inside. The two of them were amazed that the club was upscale enough for a suit and tie crowd but still maintained a hood vibe for those who like to rock jeans and Jordan's. There were two floors; the first level had a huge bar and a mini restaurant built in one while the second floor contained nothing but spacious VIP sections. The vibe was smooth and there was no drama in sight as the DJ played 2 Chainz ft Ty Dolla Sign and Trey Songz and Jhene Aiko's *It's A Vibe.*

"This shit is nice." Janae said, looking around the club, admiring its décor. She was very impressed and seen why the club had made a name for itself. They both took a seat at the bar and ordered shots of Crown Apple.

"Hell yea. And the deejay is showing out as well." Lailah smiled as she listened to Janae sing along with the words to Jhene Aiko's verse. She loved hearing her friend sing because she had a real nice voice.

"Hey, there pretty lady." A deep voice came up from behind and whispered in Lailah's ear.

CHAPTER 6

*Z*ion spotted Lailah as soon as she walked inside the club. It was his goal to surprise her because she had been on his mind heavy since they first met. Lailah was looking like a whole meal in her outfit and Zion quickly went in and made his move.

"Hey there. You neva told me your name." Lailah looked deep into his dark brown eyes. She was obviously attracted to him by the vibe she was giving off.

"I'm Zion." He responded. He flashed his Colgate smile and shook her hand.

"This is my best friend Janae. Janae, this is Zion." Lailah introduced.

"Would you ladies like to come up to the VIP section? Way less crowded." Zion offered. He could sense Lailah's hesitation but after a minute, she agreed. Zion took Lailah by the hand and led her and Janae upstairs to the second floor. The private VIP section was very spacious with a white curtain that surrounded the outside while inside there was white furniture positioned against the wall and a pool table that sat in the middle. Zion could see the look on Lailah's face and could tell she was impressed.

"Have a seat anywhere you like. This is my partner Derell. Derell, this is Lailah and her bestie Janae." Zion watched all three of them shake hands then took a seat next to Lailah.

"This place is poppin'. The owner made a damn good investment." Lailah commented as she looked around, scanning the club and its decor.

"Thank you. I wanted nothing but the best for this place." Zion replied.

Lailah's eyebrows shot up. "Wait, you're the owner?" She questioned with disbelief.

"I am." Zion replied.

"This is your place? Stop lying." Lailah said playfully. It was her first time meeting a guy who appeared to have his shit completely together. Plus, she loved the fact that Zion wasn't cocky nor did he come off as an asshole.

"I have no reason to lie." Zion stated, humbled. "This is my joint." He smiled proudly.

"That's what's up," Janae commented.

"Yeah." Lailah blushed slightly while staring into Zion's eyes.

"So did the two of you have a good day today?" Zion changed the subject. He motioned for one of his servers to come over then asked, "What are you ladies drinking?"

"Crown Apple." Janae answered for the both of them.

"Good choice." Derell chimed in. Janae smiled then redirected her attention to the crowd inside the club.

Zion nodded his head then advised his employee to bring them two bottles of their selected liquor.

"We had a great day." Lailah answered. "We hung out and had lunch earlier."

"Nothing like some good seafood." Zion stated nonchalantly. When Lailah's lips parted but no words came out, he knew she had put two and two together. He wanted her to know he had been the one that paid their check at Mae's, but he didn't want to appear arrogant in the process. Yes, he wanted credit because he liked it; but at the same time, he was hoping not to turn Lailah off. She didn't seem like the type to stroke a nigga's ego.

"Thank you for paying for our meals. You didn't have to do that." Lailah finally responded.

"But I wanted to. And I'm glad you enjoyed them." Zion said in a sincere tone. He was a true believer in what's meant to be will find its way, which is why he opted not to make himself known when he seen Lailah at his restaurant. Zion wanted to be patient, but he was also willing to earn Lailah's attention at any cost. Since this was their third time being at the same place at the same time, he decided that tonight was his final chance. Their server returned with two large bottles of Crown Apple and four shot glasses. She sat them down on the table then asked Zion if he needed anything else.

"Not at this moment." He replied politely.

"Um, I doubt we'll even drink half of that." Lailah said nervously.

"And I believe it... but I'm a generous host." He smiled, causing her to blush again. "Figured I'd take a shot with you, although Hennessey is more of my speed." Zion opened the bottle and poured everyone a shot. They all clinked their glasses together and took the liquor to the head. "So, Ms. Lailah. Tell me how is it that we keep running in to each other all of a sudden." Zion gave Lailah a lustful look that read he was definitely into her.

"You tell me. You ain't stalking me, are you?" Lailah batted her long natural eyelashes at Zion. The wall she had to protect her heart was being broken by Zion's charm. It was hard to resist Zion because he didn't come at her like the guys she was used to.

"Nah, that type of shit is pathetic and sad. If you stalking somebody, yo ass got serious problems." Zion chuckled. He pulled out a rolled backwood and a lighter from his pocket. "You smoke?"

"Nun but big gas." Lailah flirted. She watched Zion do the honors and took the first few pulls before he handed it to her. Not one to be outdone, Lailah took a few hits and handed it to Derell.

"Aight, I hear you beautiful." Zion challenged. He didn't know if she was indeed a smoker or if she was just trying to impress him, but either way, he was feeling it. "Besides working in retail, is there anything else that takes up your time?"

"I attend UNCW full-time as well."

"Word? What's ya major?" Zion asked. If he wasn't already drawn to Lailah before, knowing about her education made him even more interested in her.

"English. I have one more year as an undergrad." Lailah explained as she took a couple more hits from the backwood. Immediately, the loud began to take over and she was higher than she had ever been. Her eyes got low and her pussy throbbed from the way Zion was looking at her.

"Tapping out already?" Zion teased. He noticed how red her eyes had gotten in just a short amount of time. He smiled when Lailah shook her head yes and admired her honesty. "So what's your plans after graduation?" Zion didn't know what it was about Lailah, but he wanted to know more about her. He was enjoying their conversation and was happy that he had ran into her again. Derell and Janae also appeared to have their own vibe going; this somewhat shocked Zion because Derell was hard as hell on women and often came off as cut-throat when he met them. He watched as Derell took Janae by the hand, assisted her out of her seat, then led her to one of the free pool tables in the corner.

"I'm applying for Grad school but don't know where yet." Lailah responded.

"Do ya thang Queen. There is no limit when it comes to your dreams. I commend you for wanting to pursue your education even further." Zion complimented. Lailah was already showing him that she could be the full package.

"Thanks. It's a true pain in the ass but I'm trying. Have you already graduated?"

"I got my associates from Wake Tech and then came down here to reside. My attention span is hella short, but I wanted to have some type of degree under my belt." Zion explained. Asking about important details of his life is what separated Lailah from the other girls he dealt with in his past; half of the women in his past didn't even know he had a degree.

"School ain't for everybody. But you should be proud of yourself that you didn't give up." Lailah stated. She looked over and seen Janae and Derell hitting it off as they played a game of pool. They were both flirting with each other like high school sweethearts. The DJ switched the mood and played R. Kelly's *Slow Wind,* which was one of Lailah's favorite's songs.

"I love this song." Lailah stated standing.

Zion licked his lips while admiring her. "Really? What you know about this?"

Lailah smiled seductively then eased down on his lap and started rotating her hips. She didn't know if it was because she was high or if it was because she felt comfortable with Zion, but she felt she could let loose and he wouldn't pass judgment.

"Damn." Zion held onto her hips as his dick began rising in his pants. Lailah was not only turning him on, she was *guaranteeing* that she would be the next woman he had in his bed. Lailah was in her own little world until something clicked inside her head, and she quickly ended her mini dance session.

"Why you stop?" Zion was enjoying Lailah's slow grind until she ceased her movements out of nowhere.

"Mm, I forgot where I was for a moment." Lailah felt embarrassed because she didn't want to give off the wrong impression. The loud had her feeling some type of way and had made her bold as hell.

"You were doing a great job actually. You already started and it would only be right if you'd finished." Zion was laying it on thick and was testing her confidence. To make the deal even sweeter, he reached inside his pocket and pulled out a thick wad of money that contained nothing but hundred-dollar bills. He then peeled off fifteen bills out of his stack and handed it to Lailah. Without saying another word, Lailah got up and stood directly in front of Zion, moving her hips in sync with the music. Zion was captivated by how well Lailah was dancing and knew the loud had a lot to do with it. Her body was in tune with the lyrics of the song and he savored every minute of it. Lailah sat back down on his lap and began slow grinding against his hard dick. Zion couldn't help himself and used both his hands to hold her hips as she gave him the private dance of a lifetime. Halfway through the dance, it had crossed his mind if Lailah had ever been a stripper by the way she was throwing it at him. Zion could only imagine how well Lailah could ride his dick and wanted to fuck her right then and there. Zion held his composure and remained a gentleman for the remainder of his personal dance.

"Damn, you was holding back on a nigga. Wassup with

that?" Zion stated. He was sad once the song had ended but was happy when Lailah chose to sit back on his lap. He could tell she was beginning to feel more comfortable around him, which was a good thing in his eyes.

"I didn't want you to get the wrong idea of me. I'm not like these whores around here. I do have morals and whatnot." Lailah answered.

"Oh, I can tell. And it's a huge turn-on. Your goals and aspirations alone set you apart from these washed up chicks. But your beauty is what takes my breath away." Zion gently held Lailah's chin as he gazed into her light brown eyes. It was one of his favorite features about her that secretly tugged at his heartstrings. To him, Lailah was the true definition of one of God's best creations he put on earth.

"Thank you for the compliment." Lailah cheesed, revealing her bright white smile.

It was after 4 a.m. when Zion and Derell escorted Lailah and Janae back to their vehicle. Zion couldn't remember the last time he held a long conversation with a female that felt real and wasn't forced. He uncovered Lailah's good sense of humor along with her personality being laid-back.

"Will I have to take my chances before seeing you again or you gonna let me take you to lunch or dinner sometime soon?" Zion questioned. He handed Lailah his black iPhone XR and watched her program her number into his phone. Zion took his phone back and gave Lailah a huge hug and closed her car door behind her.

"Hit me and find out." Lailah responded as Janae slowly backed away and pulled off onto the street. Zion smirked at her flirty comment and watched their car drive off until it was no longer in sight.

"So you feeling her I see?" Derell teased as him and Zion hopped inside his grey BMW 540i.

"She might be the one brah."

"Shit, you serious?"

"More serious than I've ever been about anything." Zion answered without hesitation.

CHAPTER 7

*I*t was the next morning when Zion opened his eyes and did his morning stretch across his king-sized bed. The short amount of time he spent with Lailah the night before had him feeling things he couldn't explain. Zion wanted to take his time with getting to know Lailah because he didn't want to screw up a potentially good thing. Lailah was worth the wait and had possessed the many qualities that he looked for in a partner. Zion fumbled underneath his covers until he found his phone. He decided to shoot Lailah a text to see how she felt.

Zion: Good morning queen. I hope you slept well.

Lailah: Good morning to you too. And I did. Wbu?

Zion: It was aight. What's your plans for today?

Lailah: I'ma visit my mom for a lil while and come back to town. I rarely get Saturdays off, so I plan on enjoying it while I can.

Zion: Cool. Drive safe. Maybe I can see you later.

Lailah: I think we can make that happen.

Zion: Bet. See you later beautiful.

Zion was relieved when Lailah agreed to meet him

because his heart was racing the whole time while he waited for her reply. Lailah was the first female who made Zion nervous to be around her. There was something about Lailah that made him want to finally open up and settle down. Zion did one more final stretch and walked towards his master bathroom to take a shower.

He lived in a two-story light brick home that had an ocean view. His five bedroom, four and a half bath was furnished with nothing but modern touches. He stepped inside his wide walk-in shower and adjusted the temperature before getting in. He allowed the warm water to rain down his head and unto his back. There was a gut feeling that instantly came over him that he just couldn't shake. After being in the shower for over an hour, he got dressed and went downstairs into his chef made kitchen. There was a huge island that rested in the middle of the kitchen with dark cabinets and quartz countertops. Zion was a guy of multiple talents with cooking being one of them. He took out a box of Aunt Jemima pancake/waffle mix, a pack of bacon, and sausage links. Once he finished making a couple waffles with his sides of meat, he took a seat at his breakfast nook and thumbed through Snapchat. Getting bored with his followers, he looked on his main menu and added Lailah as a friend. After Lailah accepted his request, he looked at a snap she recently posted. It was a picture of Lailah showing how long her hair was with the caption saying, "Length Check." Zion was in awe when he seen Lailah's hair stopping at the middle of her back.

"*Shrinkage is a mothafucka.*" Zion said to himself. His thoughts got interrupted as an incoming call came through.

"Wassup Ky?" Zion greeted.

"We gotta code nine."

"I'll be there after while." Zion hung up feeling enraged.

Code 9 meant that someone had stolen from him and that

was an unforgiveable sin in Zion's eyes. At this point, Zion was ready to go to war but kept his cool until he heard the full story. He put his dishes in the dishwasher and ran outside to his garage and left out driving his Lexus Gs 350. Zion made the hour drive to Myrtle Beach, SC using only backroads and shortcuts. Different scenarios plagued his mind the entire drive. Zion drove into the small neighborhood that housed only single and double-wides. He stopped at the end of the road and turned into the yard that housed a yellow double-wide. He slammed his car door and jogged up the short pair of steps and entered the home. If looks could kill, everyone that was in Zion's eyesight would've dropped dead. Kyron, who was Zion's other partner, and three guys-- Preston, Mark and Trey-- were spread out through the kitchen and living room.

"How much was stolen?" Zion asked Kyron while looking at the three boys with an ill feeling.

"Eighty keys." Kyron answered with a straight face. He looked over at the three guys who looked to be guilty.

"Hmph, and all three of you were here when the robbery took place, correct? And yet not one of you niggas did shit, huh?" Zion directed his attention towards Preston, Mark and Trey, who all gave nothing but excuses. After hearing each of the guy's story, Zion had only one thing on his mind.

"Huge mistake." Zion shook his head. His gut was telling him that one of the guys was lying and he didn't have the patience to figure out which one. One of the things Zion didn't tolerate was a liar and someone had to answer for his loss. He smoothly pulled his weapon from the waistband of his pants.

Pop! Pop! Pop!

Zion gave nothing but headshots to each guy before they could say another word. He tucked his .22 in the back of his pants and looked over at Kyron, who was unbothered by what just happened. Kyron was just as upset about the situation as Zion, if not more. Kyron was a twenty-four-year-old hustler who had a lot of personal problems within his family. He had been working for Zion for almost five years and had earned his status with massive amounts of weight he moved. Kyron was out of town meeting with their connect when the alleged robbery had taken place. Kyron had his doubts about the three guys from the start but decided not to question Zion's judgment.

"Get rid of these niggas and hit me when you find out something." Zion ordered and left back out the house. Zion wanted answers and wasn't going to sleep until he got even. It was the principle of it all to answer why he was pissed beyond measure. Zion had more than enough product that could replace what he lost but that wasn't his issue. He got back on highway 17 feeling enraged, hatred, vengeful, and bitter all in one. This was his first time losing product as being a dealer who was high in status. He looked at his gas needle and pulled into the Exxon gas station in Bolivia. When he parked his car beside a pump, he did a doubletake as he saw two females engaged in a fight.

"What the fuck?" Zion said as he noticed one of the girls being Lailah. He kind of felt bad for Lailah's opponent because she was receiving a brutal beatdown. All of a sudden, a county sheriff car pulled up and put both girls in handcuffs. "Fuck," Zion blurted. He watched as a familiar face stepped out of the patrol car. "Ayo John, it's cool. The one in the pink and white is with me!" Zion yelled as he approached them.

John shook his head then released Lailah from her handcuffs. "Keep her out of trouble," he ordered.

"I got her." Zion replied.

"You just gon' let that bitch go?" The other woman screamed as John proceeded to place her in the back of the car. "That's bullshit!" She ranted. "Fuck you Lailah, trifflin' ass bitch!"

"You know what?" Lailah took a step towards the car.

"Lailah." Zion spoke, grabbing her arm. "Let it go."

Lailah took a deep breath, trying to calm her nerves then slowly exhaled. "Thanks for that." She stated sincerely.

"Who was that?" Zion asked. He took her by the hand and guided her towards her car. It was usually a turn-off for Zion to see females fight but the way Lailah handled her business only peeked his interests more.

"My bum-ass lil sister. I made a promise to myself that I was gonna beat that bitch on sight when I saw her." Lailah huffed. Other than a few scratches on her arm, she had no other injuries present.

"Damn, well I see you conquered. What she do to deserve that?"

"Enough..."

CHAPTER 8

"*D*amn" was all Zion could say when Lailah gave him the backstory of her and her sister's relationship.

"Mhmm. I can't stand that bitch." Lailah fumed.

Earlier, she was in the middle of pumping gas when she spotted her sister coming out of the store. Lailah was a bomb waiting to explode and she didn't give her school career a second thought. It wasn't until when she felt the handcuffs being placed around her wrists that reality had finally sunk in. Lailah was thankful when Zion came in and saved the day from her being hauled off to jail.

"I see. You was giving her the business. Who taught you how to fight like that?" Zion was extremely curious.

"I would play fight with my older cousins growing up. Plus, they couldn't take me being sensitive. They said I was soft like cotton." Lailah explained.

"Well they definitely taught you well. I don't want the rest of your evening to be spoiled, so you wanna go get sum to eat?" Zion suggested. He couldn't take seeing her get in any trouble, especially since her schooling was on the line.

"Yea, that's fine. You ever been to *J Michael Philly?*"

"Have I? Hell yea. I see you got good taste. I'll lead the way." Zion joked. He gave Lailah a kiss on her cheek and watched her get inside her car. He then hopped in his vehicle and waited for Lailah to follow behind him before driving on to the main high way.

"Lord, what am I getting myself into?" Lailah said to herself. She thumbed through her playlist on her phone and played Jhene Aiko's *While We're Young* as she followed Zion back to town. Lailah was slightly confused on where her and Zion stood. She didn't want to begin a new relationship when she still wasn't completely over her ex. The chemistry between her and Zion was undeniable, one that had grew within the short amount of time they spent together. Once they arrived at their destination, Lailah parked her car in the space next to Zion's and got out.

"I ain't been here in a min." Zion stated. He looked Lailah up and down, admiring her. There was no doubt that she could dress her ass off. Today, she had worn some light denim stressed jean jeggings from American Eagle with a white and pink striped crop top with white converses. Zion was getting the best of both worlds with Lailah. She carried herself with class but had a little bit of hood in her at the same time.

"Yea, me neither. I would try to save money from going out to eat cause that shit adds up." Lailah said. They sat down at a table that rested against the wall.

"You know what you getting?" Zion asked, looking over his menu.

"Mmmm, yep. I'ma try their salad today." Lailah answered. She was feeling a little nervous being that this was her first date with Zion.

"Good evening guys, my name is Erin and I'll be your

server. Can I start you off with some drinks?" The woman asked.

"Can I have an ice water with extra lemon.?" Lailah replied.

"And I'll have a sweet tea." Zion said.

"Are y'all ready to order or do you need a few more minutes?"

"No ma'am. I want the Philly cheese steak with no veggies. Whole please." Zion stated.

"I'll have an order of your cheese sticks and chef salad with no peppers or olives." Lailah said.

"Alright, I'll bring you your drinks and put your order in." The waitress took their menus and trailed off towards the kitchen.

"Did you and that cop go to school together?" Lailah asked. The fact that the officer just let her go by Zion's command had her thinking. She wanted to see if he was going to be all the way honest with her. There was a short pause between them before Zion finally answered her.

"He's on my payroll." Zion confessed. As soon as those words left his mouth, he seen a sad look appear on Lailah's face. Their waitress came back and served them their dinks and informed them that their food would be out shortly. She left as quickly as she came and went to go check on her other customers.

"I promised myself that I would never date a dude who's in the game. *Ever.*" Lailah sat back and folded her arms against her chest. She blew out a long sigh and took sip from her water.

"But?" Zion was hoping that she would overlook his situation.

"What do you specialize in?" Lailah asked, avoiding his comment. Her intuition was telling her to get up and leave but for some reason, her legs wouldn't move.

"Coke."

"Along with bud I assume." Lailah finished his sentence. Lailah was glad to see their waitress heading towards them with their food in hand. The tension was extremely thick and Lailah's meal was the only thing that could calm her nerves in that moment. "And to answer your question from earlier, I don't date men in your field for many reasons. Me and you both know what two outcomes that shit leads to." Lailah was upset to find out the truth behind Zion but she wasn't surprised. She knew she'd be taking a huge risk if she chose to continue dealing with Zion.

"It's not like I'ma be doing it forever. I'm soon 'bout to wrap this shit up." Zion assured.

"That's what they all say." Lailah scoffed. She rolled her eyes at his last comment as she continued to eat her mozzarella sticks.

"I'm serious. I have a few more businesses I'll be investing into. After that, I'm good." Zion completely underestimated Lailah's level of intelligence. He was trying his best to convince her so she could be more at ease, but the expression on her face was clear that she wasn't buying it.

"I hear you. Next subject. How many serious relationships have you been in?" Lailah switched gears in their conversation before she said something she might end up regretting.

"To be honest, none. I was never set on being tied down to someone unless she was worth it. I fucked around with this one girl named Toree for four years, going on five, but even with her, I told her in the beginning to not catch feelings. She did anyway and I cut her off. She was nothing more than just a fuck to me." Zion layed everything on the line for Lailah.

"Mm. So you never been in love is what you're saying?" Lailah pressed. She didn't know whether that was a good thing or a bad thing.

"I can't say I have. Every female I dealt with was only about the material things."

"And I wonder why." Lailah was still aggravated with Zion but the look he was giving her softened her heart.

"What about you?" Zion ignored Lailah's smart comment. If anything, her attitude and feistiness was turning him on.

"I been in three serious relationships between high school and now. My recent ex kept fucking around during our relationship until I finally gathered enough courage to walk away. If I didn't give a shit about my record or my schooling, I woulda fucked that nigga and his hoe up. No cap." Lailah expressed while taking a few bites of her salad.

"But you ain't gotta worry about that now. You deserve a man whose gonna value you in every way. I'm ready to open up and see what the future holds for the both of us. Just like everyone else in the world, I wanna get married and have kids too, shit. But I'm only gonna do that with the right one." Zion said.

"So you think I'm that one?"

"That's what I'm trynna find out." Zion smiled.

"How many kids you want?" Lailah was taken back at how Zion was showing his soft side. Behind all the thuggish layers he carried, he was nothing but a true sweetheart underneath.

"Two. A boy and a girl." Zion responded. "You?"

"The same but I want my girl first." Lailah informed. "And the reason being is cause I just want to get her out the way first. I'm not one of those females whose gonna keep trying and trying for a specific gender. Hell no." Lailah added. Zion almost choked on his sandwich from laughing so hard.

"Wow. Okay then. Your reasoning is understandable." Zion cleared his throat. He still wasn't clear on where they both stood or whether they would keep seeing each other or not. The mood was finally at a good place and he didn't want to ruin it by questioning her about their status. The way his pride was set up, Zion took a deep breath and asked anyway. "So where do we stand now that you know my real occupation?"

"We can just take it one day at a time. You know I'm new to this type of situation so bear with me. And word of advice, *don't* fuck up." Lailah gave him a death stare.

"I won't. I've been waiting a long time for a female like you." Zion promised.

They continued to talk about each of their plans for the future for the remainder of their meal. After Zion paid the bill, he walked Lailah to her car and gave her a hug.

"Call me when you've made it home," Zion instructed before he got in his vehicle.

"I will." Lailah answered before driving off.

Toree bit her inner cheek as she watched the exchange between Lailah and Zion. She felt like vomiting after seeing Zion being intimate with another woman. *"I'll see you soon bitch."* Toree snickered as she watched Zion and Lailah pull off in their cars. Toree wasn't about to let another female come in and stop her funds.

CHAPTER 9

*I*t was five minutes after three in the afternoon when Lailah was placing packages of soap into their correct spot. She had less than an hour to go until her shift was over and she was beyond ready to leave. Being the department manager over health and beauty aids had its days. Dealing with rude customers was one of the small issues Lailah could ignore. It was the fakeness and constant drama with her co-workers that made Lailah want to quit every other day. Knowing that her graduation was less than a year away was the only thing that kept her going; besides the fact she needed the money.

"Excuse me," a woman's voice asked from behind.

"Yes, can I help you?" Lailah turned around.

"Yea, you can help me out by staying the fuck away from my man!" The woman seethed.

"I'm sorry? Do I know you?" Lailah was confused and felt the lady had her mistaken for someone else. Her first reaction was to beat the woman's ass and ask questions later, but she couldn't afford to lose her job.

"Don't worry 'bout who I am. You just stay the fuck away from Zion! He's playing yo ass anyway."

Whap!

The woman slapped Lailah across the face and grabbed her by the hair as she shoved Lailah into her work cart nearby. The woman then threw bottles of shampoo in Lailah's direction until she seen one of Lailah's co-workers running in her direction. The woman quickly ran away from the scene, leaving Lailah on the floor struggling to get up.

"Oh my goodness! Lailah, are you alright?!" Julie, one of Lailah's co-workers, came to her aide. She helped Lailah to her feet and walked her to the back towards the breakroom. Lailah took a seat at the table as Julie handed her a small mirror to spot any injuries. There was a small cut near one of Lailah's eyebrows. While Julie went to go retrieve a band-aid, Lailah took out her phone and sent Zion a text.

Lailah: Nigga you need to learn how to control yo hoes! And to think I was gonna give you a chance? You got me fucked up.

When Zion didn't respond, it only fueled Lailah's anger even more. "Lying ass nigga." She grumbled.

News of Lailah's incident had spread like wildfire but worked out in her favor when her supervisor allowed her to go home early. Lailah went to her locker and grabbed her keys and purse. She swiped her badge through the time clock and headed out the door. When she saw Zion coming her way, she rolled her eyes and continued to walk towards her car.

"Lailah, I know you hear me calling you! What the hell happened?" Zion urged. He stood in front of Lailah's car door, purposely blocking her from getting in.

"Why don't you ask ya bitch!" Lailah yelled. She tried pushing Zion out her way, but it was no use. Her strength was nothing compared to his muscles and body weight.

"Hey, calm down. I can't fix shit if you won't tell me

what's wrong." Zion grabbed Lailah's small waist and looked into her eyes. "I'm listening."

"This girl came in my department demanding that I stop seeing you. Who is she? Putting my mothafuckin' job in jeopardy and shit. What the fuck Zion?" Lailah tried to fight against his touch but the way he was handling her made her pussy moist.

"Was she light-skin and had black hair?" Zion asked even though he knew the answer to his question. When Lailah shook her head yes, he quickly took out his phone and sent a text. "If you want yo licks back, come with me."

"You damn right I want my licks back. But let's make this shit quick because I have other plans." Lailah decided not to argue against Zion's offer. She wasn't the type of female to let things slide. Lailah got into Zion's car and opted not to say anything the whole ride. She still blamed Zion for the whole encounter she had earlier and was having second thoughts about their relationship. Twenty minutes later, Lailah looked around her surroundings once they got to their destination. She got out and walked up towards the small warehouse building that was located deep in the woods. Zion slid the door back and motioned for Lailah to walk inside. In the middle of the room, Toree was bound to a wooden chair where her arms and legs were tied together. She had sweat and make-up running down her face.

"Is this her?" Zion asked Lailah. He went over to Toree and snatched the duct tape off that covered her mouth. Toree let out a low scream.

"Yea." Lailah took a few steps towards Toree and shook her head. "Yo hoe ass got a lot of nerve coming to my place of work and showing yo ass. You shoulda stayed in yo place and worried less about what I got going on." Lailah spat. Now that she had the upper hand, she made sure to give Toree a piece of her mind.

"Bitch, fuck you and yo punk-ass job!" Toree yelled.

Bop! Bop!

Lailah punched Toree across the face. "Fuck me? Nah bitch, fuck you! Don't be mad at me cause yo pussy ain't worth shit anymore!" Lailah stated. Lailah backhanded Toree, feeling like her point had been made. "I'm through with this hoe." Lailah said to Zion and walked back outside.

"You did this to ya self." Zion said to Toree. He looked at Derell who placed the silencer on his pistol and put a few slugs into Toree's dome. Zion walked out feeling no type of way and was glad that Toree was now only a memory.

"So this the type of bullshit I gotta put up with?" Lailah asked, breaking the silence between them.

"I'm sorry Lai. Had I known she was that crazy, I woulda never fucked with her from the start." Zion reasoned. The signs of extreme jealousy had always been there from Toree but Zion had chosen to neglect them.

"I ain't trynna hear that bullshit." Lailah waved him off. She was still pissed at Zion for putting her in that type of predicament. "She better never come for me again."

"I promise she won't." Zion stated coldly.

Once they arrived back at the Wal-Mart parking lot, Lailah stormed out without saying another word with Zion jogging behind her. Zion caught Lailah by the arm and pulled her into his embrace.

"C'mon now. Stop trynna fight me. Let me make it up to you." Zion pleaded.

"I'll think about it. Can you let me go please?" Lailah ordered. As soon as Zion released his grip, she got into her car and sped off. Lailah was yet again stuck between what her mind and heart wanted. She didn't know if Zion was being real or was just messing with her head. Lailah felt a small headache coming on as she drove across town to Janae's apartment.

"*W*ell lookie here." Janae greeted as she opened her door so Lailah could walk in.

"Hey to you too." Lailah said as she went straight towards the kitchen. She pulled out a pack of Oreo's, pancake mix, and oil.

"What done happened now for you to come in here to make some fried Oreos?" Janae asked. She took a seat at the bar and prepared herself for the worst.

"I don't think me and Zion is gonna make it."

"What? Y'all just started talking. Damn."

"And that's the problem. He already got a bitch coming at me sideways and shit. I can't fucking deal." Lailah said as she stirred up her pancake mix in a bowl.

"Pause. He did what now?" Janae couldn't believe what she was hearing. She felt bad for her friend in that moment because it was as if life had kept throwing her curve balls nonstop.

"Yea girl. She came to my job and everything. She put her damn hands on me too, but I got my hits back thanks to Zion. But that nigga ain't off the hook." Lailah vented. She placed her battered Oreos in the hot grease and licked her lips in anticipation.

"I agree with you, I do. But let me ask you this. Were they still fucking with each other when she made the scene at your workplace?"

"Nah, they been broke up. Plus he said they wasn't in a relationship and she was only his piece of pussy when needed." Lailah said. "You want some?" Lailah asked, pointing at her Oreos.

"Daggone right I do. But I think you should cut him some slack Lai." Janae proposed. She seen a different glow in Lailah when it came to her being with Zion.

"How many you gone eat?" Lailah dismissed Janae's suggestion. All she wanted in that moment was to indulge in one of her favorite type of sweets and to forget about Zion for the rest of the night.

"As many as I want in my house." Janae teased.

"My bad Nae." Lailah sighed. "That nigga got me fucked up.."

"Naw, that nigga got you."

CHAPTER 11

*A*lmost a week had passed since Zion had heard from Lailah. Not being able to see her, let alone hearing her voice, was making him stir crazy. Zion thought it'd be best to give her some space, but he didn't think she would take this long. He called and texted both morning and night but she'd never reply. Zion had to soon come up with a plan to get back in Lailah's good graces.

"Aye brah, you still bugging bout ol' girl?" Derell asked. They were both sitting on the couch watching the sports channel when Derell took notice of Zion's slight mood change.

"Hell yea. She's been avoiding my calls and texts. Shit starting to get on my nerves. I apologized Ion know how many times. I still don't see how it's my fault tho." Zion vented. He knew Lailah had him wide-open and had him acting like a child yearning for some attention.

"And what make it so bad, you ain't even had the pussy yet, and she got you over here pouting and shit." Derell laughed. "But I ain't gone say *'I told you so,'* but look, you can surprise her tonight at the open mic showcase. Janae told me that they were performing together. After the show, maybe she'll hear you out." Derell stated.

"What the hell you two got going on?" Zion questioned. Knowing Derell's history with women, it would take a miracle for him to be with one girl.

"Not shit. We decided we're not gonna put a title on us. I told her I ain't ready to commit just yet. I still got a lot of lust that needs to be brought out." Derell said, rubbing his chest. Derell liked Janae a lot but her bratty personality was one he couldn't take.

"Mm. You must be still fucking that Latino broad." Zion thumbed through social media checking his personal messages.

"Her and Simone's fat ass. Can't let 'em go just yet." Derell answered truthfully. He was content with the options he had and had no plans on being cuffed anytime soon. "But I got that info you been waiting on. I found out who was behind that hit the other night." Derell looked at Zion's blank expression and took that as his cue to continue talking. "And you not gonna believe who it is." Derell took another pause. "Orion."

"I'm not surprised. That nigga always been a punk-ass bitch." Zion said in a low tone.

"Well, I been watching him for a lil while now. The keys he took ended up being his major come-up. Before that, he was your average nickeling and diming nigga struggling on the block. His partner, well old partner now, told me that Preston, Mark, and Trey were a part of his circle. Apparently, he used them lil niggas as pawns because he got a whole new set of niggas working for him now." Derell informed. He looked over at Zion ,who soaked up all his information like a sponge. Zion had that look in his eyes that Derell knew all too well.

"He been in competition with me ever since we were in

diapers. He just don't know he signed off on his death warrant." Zion brought his attention back down to his phone.

"Well, whenever you ready to make ya move, just say word." Derell replied. He'd been feening for a while to body a nigga because it gave him a rush he couldn't explain. Toree's murder was quick and clean; he found no pleasure in it. He like seeing those who crossed him or his family suffer, that's what he had planned for Orion and the others. "But how's ya mom's progress been coming along?" He questioned.

"I been meaning to go by there and visit. Just been slipping my mind and shit."

"Well she gonna make it thru. No doubt about that." Derell commented. He changed the subject knowing Zion's mom was a sensitive subject for him. "Also, I got word from Janae that you and Lailah's birthdays are close together."

"For y'all two to only be fuck buddies, y'all sure talk about personal topics." Zion shook his head. "But how close we talking?"

"A day apart."

"Quit capping nigga." Zion said. It gave him the answers to why Lailah acted the way she did at certain moments.

"I'm serious. Now you can plan something for you and her instead of sitting in this house like a senior citizen and shit." Derell joked.

"Fuck you nigga. Ain't nun wrong with just relaxing on your birthday. But shit, I already got an idea tho. One she won't be able to turn down."

"I hope it goes well for you." Derell hoped. It was his first time seeing Zion getting serious with a female. He was low-key proud of the man Zion was becoming and would later down the road follow into his footsteps.

"What time the show start?" Zion asked. He wanted to be sure to get there on time.

"At nine. You wanna ride with me or you gone drive?"

"I'll drive just in case tonight goes my way." Zion smirked.

"Aight brah, I'll meet you there later on. Good luck." Derell stood up and gave Zion a half hug before leaving.

Zion went to his kitchen and grabbed a bottle of water. He had three hours to kill and decided to smoke a couple of blunts and chill until it was time for him to get ready. He was nervous about seeing Lailah and only hoped for the best. Zion wasn't used to rejection, but in a way, it made him want to be the man he needed to be for Lailah. He sat down on his couch and placed his rolling tray on his lap as he rolled and pearled two thick blunts. Zion flipped through his channels until he came across one of his favorite sitcoms, *Martin*. He puffed on the loud as Lailah clouded his mind. Somewhere along the line, his mother had entered his thoughts and blew his high. Zion's mother Karen had been in rehab for two years and he only seen her a total of three times. Since she started the program, Zion still felt hatred towards his mother but had forgiven her to the point where he would offer to give her help. He knew he needed to make amends, he just didn't know how.

When it finally came time for Zion to get ready, he took a thirty-minute shower and dressed down in a white Nautica muscle shirt, tan pants, and a pair of Sperry sneakers. Zion wasn't the type to be flashy, so he avoided drawing unwanted attention to himself. He said a quick prayer and headed out the door.

CHAPTER 12

Zion drove downtown until he reached his destination. When he turned in the parking lot, he spotted Derell's car and parked beside him. He got out and walked inside the building and seen Derell sitting at the bar.

"I see you made it." Derell said as Zion approached him. "I got us seats near the front." Derell got up and led Zion to their table.

"It's about time they renovated this place. All the money they make throughout the year." Zion commented, looking around. "Do you know what slot they're in?"

"Nah, that's the one thing Janae purposely kept a secret." Derell chuckled.

The male host came on stage and greeted everyone that was in attendance. He said a few quotes of his own to warm up the audience and then introduced the first speaker of the night.

Almost two hours had passed, and it was getting towards the end of the show as Zion's patience started to wear thin. He began to think that Lailah and Janae had cancelled their performance at the last minute.

"As always, we saved the best for last. This is their first time performing, please welcome Janae and Lailah to the stage!" The announcer said, clapping his hands along with the crowd. Zion's eyes lit up as he watched Lailah take her place and grabbed the mic. The light grey bodycon dress she was wearing showed off her athletic figure. Her hair was styled into a tight bun that Zion was feeling. Janae started playing her guitar as Lailah later joined in reciting her poem. Zion could feel every emotion in Lailah's special piece. Her poem was raw, deep, and moving, and had the crowd snapping their fingers at every other line she spoke. It tugged at Zion's heartstrings that made him want her even more. When Lailah was finished, the audience gave her a roaring applause while some people shouted "Encore!" Zion watched Lailah and Janae give each other a hug and exited off stage. The announcer came back on and said his final remarks and upcoming events. Zion searched throughout the crowd until he finally spotted Lailah and Janae walking out the door.

"Y'all in a hurry or sumthing?" Zion asked when he caught up to Lailah. To his surprise, she looked excited to see him.

"Yea, my ass is hungry. Did you enjoy the show?"

"Hell yea. Y'all performance was dope. And these are for you." Zion handed Lailah a bouquet of white roses. He could tell she still felt some type of way but she ended up giving him a smile.

"Thank you, they're beautiful." Lailah replied as she took a sniff from her flowers.

"Can we talk, possibly over dinner?" Zion asked as they stood in the parking lot.

"Aight, but you got one hour." Lailah playfully rolled her eyes. She looked over at Janae, who had heard the whole conversation and gave her a hug.

"Uh, Mr. Zion. Be on your best behavior!" Janae warned.

"Yes ma'am." Zion responded. He led Lailah by the hand to his car, holding the door open. Once she was safely inside, he closed the door, moved to the driver's side, and climbed in.

"So where are we going?" Lailah wondered as Zion pulled off and went on the main highway.

"My place. Thought I'd whip up some spaghetti. I ain't had it in a long time." Zion suggested. He caught Lailah blushing in her seat because it was one of her favorite meals. Meek Mill ft Jeremih & PnB Rok's *Dangerous* blasted through the speakers as Lailah bopped her head to the music. Zion was glad she was loosening up because he wanted tonight to be special. During the drive to his home, the two of them discussed Lailah's performance and her appreciation for spoken word. Zion loved that she was multifaceted and she loved that he showed a genuine interest in the things she loved. Despite their previous run-in, they appeared to be back on good terms and common ground.

"Shit... this looks like something off TV." Lailah looked amazed as Zion pulled into his private gated home. She was speechless by the exterior of the home and could only imagine how it looked on the inside.

"You like?" Zion chuckled. It felt refreshing to him knowing he was the first one to introduce Lailah to a different lifestyle. Once they got inside, he gave her a tour throughout his home.

"I'm still trynna find the words to say. Did you decorate this yourself?" Lailah took a seat at the huge island inside the kitchen as she watched Zion take out pots and pans.

"Yea. When I was younger, I had a whole vision on what my place would look like."

"So what's the point of having so much room when it's only you?" Lailah asked. Seeing Zion cook was a plus in her book.

"I have other properties as well but this one is my favorite. I love sitting out on my balcony while having the ocean in my view. It's where I go and clear my thoughts. It's very peaceful out here."

"Holl up! No onions please." Lailah protested when she seen Zion take out a white onion from the fridge.

"You don't eat onions?" Zion chuckled.

"Eww no. I don't see how anybody can. They're disgusting. The texture and flavor. Ugh!!" Lailah made a stank face.

"Well then, your wish is my command. They're not that bad tho."

Zion placed the ground beef he had sitting in the bottom of his fridge in a skillet then grabbed a pot and filled it with cold water.

"Who taught you how to cook?"

"My mom's mom. My mother was an addict, and when I was two, she took guardianship over me. Thank God. If it wasn't for her, I woulda never made it through school." Zion admitted. His grandmother was his heart and had died a couple weeks after his high school graduation.

"I'm sorry to hear that about your mother." Lailah could see the hurt in Zion's eyes. "So what attracted you to me?" She asked, changing the subject.

"You're random as hell. Has anybody ever told you that?" Zion laughed. He was happy when she directed their conversation in a better direction because he wasn't up to discuss his mother.

"Janae yes, but she's gotten used to it."

"All bullshit aside. I've never been instantly attracted to a woman's beauty before you. Your hair is popping and those eyes make me weak. You can have anything you want just off that alone. And the fact that you're educated was the cherry on top." Zion explained. It was like Lailah was heaven sent in his eyes.

"Thank you for the compliment. I'm pretty sure you have all kinds of females throwing their pussy at you. And since you ain't never been in a serious relationship before, what's not to stop you from fucking around?" Lailah still had her doubts. She couldn't take being misled and hurt again.

"Because them bitches don't have shit I want. If all I wanted was to fuck, I wouldn't waste my time nor yours. You have the complete package. It's like God finally answered my prayers when I bumped into you that night. My ass ain't getting any younger. Shit, I was about to give up hope, but I'm grateful that I didn't."

Once their dinner was done, Zion took out a couple plates from his cabinet and made a plate for himself and Lailah. They both took their seats at the table then Zion blessed their meal.

"Wow." Lailah commented. She closed her eyes as her taste buds were on ten. "I may have to keep you around." Lailah winked.

"I ain't going nowhere." Zion shot Lailah a stern look.

"We'll see." Lailah smiled. Her clit throbbed at the way Zion was looking at her. It had been a few months since she last had sex and Zion's aggression was turning her on. "So, what are some things you like to do in your spare time? That's if you have the extra time. I know you're a *busy* man."

"I write poetry when the loud or liquor doesn't do the job. I have journals and everything. I know you may have thought I was stalking you when I came to hear you speak tonight but that wasn't the case. Yea, it was my goal to spend some time with you, but I have a hidden passion for spoken word. I like going to the beach and as you can see, I'm only a few steps away from it. I love action movies and traveling. What about you?"

"I'm a hermit. I don't like to party that much."

"Mm, coulda fooled me." Zion interjected.

"Oh hush. But seriously tho, I'm a homebody. I like shopping by myself so I can take my time. I read books and like going to the movies as well. The only place I went out of the country was to Haiti."

"Word?" Zion looked up from his plate. Haiti was one of the countries on his list to visit.

"Yea, I went with a missionary group my sophomore year in college. It was a wonderful and humbling experience. The kids there were so sweet. It broke my heart witnessing how they live day to day when you have people out here who are so ungrateful. It burns me the fuck up."

"Yea, it is sad. I read up on their history and it was some straight bullshit. They never had a chance from the jump." Zion shook his head.

"Really? Was there a specific reason?" Lailah questioned.

"Well, I love reading up on what our ancestors did for this country and the shit they had to go through. But I had to do a project for my psychology class and Haiti was a part of it."

"You ever thought about going back and getting your bachelors?"

"Yea, and I'm still debating it."

"Nothing wrong with that."

" So, I'ma ask you the same question."

"What's that?" Lailah asked curiously.

"What attracted *you* to me?" Zion asked as he collected their plates and carried them to the dishwasher.

"Nigga, Ion even know why you asked." Lailah felt like she was being put on the spot.

"Because I want to know." He stated firmly. He closed the dishwasher and then motioned for Lailah to follow him into the living room. "And that's not answering my question." Zion challenged as they settled in on the sofa.

They were so close, their legs were touching. The sexual tension Zion felt was driving him insane. He wanted to reach out and grab her, but he didn't want to overstep his boundaries. Lailah was worth the wait, even if it took everything in him to keep his composure.

"What's not to like? I love chocolate men, you have a nice smile, and your curls are so pretty... it's too cute. I can tell you keep up with your hair unlike these other niggas out here. You know how to dress, and you have a good personality to add to your looks." Lailah answered. "A female would have to be without her senses not to be attracted to you."

Zion smiled. He could no longer resist his urges; he reached over and started rubbing his hands up and down her smooth legs. His soft hands were making her pussy wetter by the second. When Zion pulled her in for a kiss, Lailah felt as if she would melt. She wrapped her arms around his neck as their tongues began having a conversation of their own. Zion pushed her down on the couch then positioned himself in between her legs. A soft moan escaped Lailah's lips as he reached up, pulling her black lace thong down and off her legs.

"Damn." Zion's dick jumped inside his pants as he looked at the creamy filling Lailah produced. His dick was aching to feel her insides, but he wanted to take his time. He heard a small gasp escape from Lailah's mouth as he began to play with her wet pussy.

"Wait! Wait. I can't." Lailah sighed. She pushed Zion off her and grabbed her panties from off the floor.

"Why? Was I being too rough or sum?" Zion asked with a confused look on his face.

"Nah, it was just right. But I gotta get up hella early in the morning for work. Plus, I don't want you to see me as that type of female. Easy come...easy go. I want us to take our time." Lailah explained.

"We been talking for a few weeks now. I don't think of

MARRIED TO A DIRTY SOUTH BOSS

you as *easy*, and I won't even if we go there." Zion tried to change her mind.

"Maybe but I just don't want to rush it."

He was sexually frustrated but he respected Lailah enough not to pressure her. "I respect your wishes and your body." He stated. "When the time is right, it'll happen."

Lailah smiled with relief. "Thank you. I appreciate that."

CHAPTER 13

*L*ailah sat at one of the desk chairs in the manager's office conversing with her store manager and a few co-workers. Her body was there but her mind was in a faraway place. She regretted stopping Zion the other night. As bad as her body craved the feeling, she didn't want to come off as being a whore. Lailah always gave herself a rule to wait for sex with a guy at least three to four months for a few reasons. Now she was beginning to think that putting a time limit on sex was a waste. She was thankful of him being a gentleman and not making her feel bad about the situation, but she knew it had to be hard for him to resist.

Zion's patience for Lailah made her feelings for him grow deeper than she anticipated. Lailah was trying hard to protect her heart but the way Zion made her feel, it was already too late. Ever since the night she left from his house, they had been texting and calling each other continuously throughout the day. Lailah loved how they could talk all day and the conversation would never get boring. Zion was outgoing, sweet, thoughtful, and kept Lailah laughing, which helped seal their bond. Lailah's phone buzzed in her pocket, triggering a smile when she seen who it was.

Zi *red heart emoji*: Missin you so much. Tell them niggas in there to wrap that shit up!

Lailah: Haha. I'm otw now. Impatient ass.

As soon as the meeting was dismissed, Lailah went to her locker and grabbed her purse. She headed out the double doors and made her way to the entrance of the store when suddenly she felt someone hug her from behind. She looked back and turned to face Zion. She kissed him on the lips then pulled away, smiling.

"How was your day?" Zion asked as he looked into her eyes.

"Stressful as always. Got inventory next week so I'll be getting mad overtime for the rest of this week and the next." Lailah informed. Inventory brought out all the craziness within the managers and their associates. It was one of the main things she hated about her job.

"I coulda helped you out with that but noooo." Zion teased.

"Oh hush. You wouldn't know what to do with me anyway." Lailah shot back. She was flirting mad hard and knew it would get under his skin.

"I'ma give you a pass this time and blame it on you being stressed." Zion shook his head. "But I gotta surprise for you." Zion wrapped one of his arms around her waist and covered her eyes with his other hand.

"A surprise? For what?" Lailah hated surprises but decided to be a good sport.

"For ending your school year on a good note. Six classes and you got all A's? I know that shit had to been rough on you." Zion replied. He couldn't wait to see the look on her face. "Almost there, just a few more steps." When he removed his hands, the expression on Lailah's face was priceless.

"Zi! Noooooo! Oh my God! Are you serious?!" Lailah yelled. She made a circle around her black 2019 Audi A5 that had a big red bow on the hood. "Zi. I can't. This is too much." Lailah covered her mouth with both her hands.

"You can still keep your old car as a backup. But you deserve it. You work so hard while being a student. I just wanna give you the world." Zion chuckled as Lailah ran and jumped into his arms. He picked her up as they shared a passionate kiss.

"Zi, it's beautiful! And you had the windows tinted too?" Lailah pointed.

"Of course. That's a must." Zion stated as he handed her the keys. "Let's go so you can get the feel of it." Zion went around to the passenger's side as Lailah pressed the unlock button.

"This is really nice." Lailah looked around at the peanut butter leather interior and the updated controls of her radio and navigation system. After turning over the engine, she adjusted her seat and rearview mirror before pulling off.

"I'm glad you like it." Zion reclined his seat back.

"I'ma stop at my place first and take a shower if that's fine with you. I'm ready to get out these work clothes." Lailah said as she came to a stop light.

"No problem. I personally like you in uniform. You make that shit look sexy as hell." Zion admitted.

"Well thank you for the compliment." Lailah said, taking off her work vest then tossing it onto the back floor board.

Lailah made the twenty-minute drive to the Avalon apartment complex. She pulled into a spot near her door and killed the engine. With Zion following behind her, she unlocked her door and ushered him inside. "It's not much but it's home." Lailah guided Zion throughout her 900 square foot one-bedroom apartment.

"It's still nice and cozy. You're doing well for ya self.

Paying your own bills while you're in school. That's hot."
Zion took a seat on the sofa.

"Would you like something to drink?" Lailah offered.

"Water please."

She walked into the kitchen then removed a bottle of
Aquafina, and then brought it to him. "Here you go." She
stated, handing him the bottle. She turned on the TV and
gave him the remote and retreated to her bedroom.

Zion browsed through the channels until he came across
the movie *Friday After Next*. He got up to take a closer look at
the pictures that were in sight. Lailah had a 42' inch flat
screen TV that rested on a black entertainment center with
photos that consisted of her and Janae throughout their
childhood. There was a solo picture of Lailah posing,
wearing a tap-dance uniform. She looked to be about six or
seven years old, which Zion thought was adorable. He went
back and took his place back on the couch and thumbed
through his Facebook. He didn't notice how fast the time
went by when Lailah came back wearing an outfit that made
his hormones go bananas. Lailah had on a light pink body-
suit with dark denim shorts and white sandals. Her hair was
damp and was styled into two French braids.

"Damn, who you trynna look good for?" Zion joked.

"I dress like this all the time. Ain't no half stepping when I
go out." Lailah walked to her kitchen counter and grabbed
her keys and purse. "You ready?"

"Yes ma'am." Zion opened the door for Lailah and closed
it behind them.

Once they hopped inside Lailah's new car, Zion
connected his Bluetooth and played Mase's *Tell Me What You
Want* as they cruised on Highway 17. He took out a vape pin
and took a few hits before he handed it over to Lailah. "I
didn't wanna mess up your new car smell."

"I woulda been fine with a regular blunt." Lailah smiled as

she took a few pulls from the pen. She went into a small coughing spell, which resulted in her eyes watering.

"Damn, sound like you trynna cough up a lung. You good?" Zion was laughing on the inside.

"I got this under control." Lailah waved him off. They continued to pass the pen back and forth until Lailah had tapped out. She felt like she was floating on top of a cloud as her stress from work had been removed.

"Rookie." Zion blurted.

"Shut yo ass up."

"And I'd love for you too." Zion said as he took another hit.

"I know." Lailah was close to giving in and submitting herself to Zion. It was as if her pussy was calling his name; she coached herself to remain strong.

"Then why keep teasing? You only making it worse on ya self."

"Cause I gotta leave you wondering. It will intensify the moment when it finally comes." Lailah explained.

"Sounds like some bullshit but whatever you say." Zion went through his playlist and tapped on Tank ft Trey Songz & Ty Dolla Sign's *When We Remix*. He caught the smile Lailah tried to hide and placed his left hand on her thigh. He could sense her urge to keep her composure and as a man of his word, he didn't go any further.

"You wanna grab a bite to eat?" Lailah managed to say. Her clit was aching like crazy as soon as Zion placed his hand on her leg. They were well into North Myrtle Beach as they passed a number of restaurants when Lailah suggested they stop somewhere.

"Sure, where you trynna go?"

"Longhorn. I love their food." Lailah answered. She made a left turn at the light and drove into the restaurant parking lot. She found a space that was near the door and turned off her engine. They got out the car and headed inside the establishment. A minute later their hostess led them to an available booth. As they walked Lailah almost stopped in her tracks. For a moment, she thought her mind was playing tricks on her. On the opposite side of the restaurant, she had witnessed Chris and the girl he had cheated with engulfed in a conversation. Chris looked as if he was the happiest man on earth from the constant laughing and smiling he was doing. The couple was too into their conversation to even notice Lailah staring at them.

"What's wrong love?" Zion looked to see what had Lailah's attention.

"Nothing, I'm good." Lailah resumed walking and took a seat at their table.

Her appetite to eat had been blown after spotting Chris and his side piece. It made her sick to her stomach now, knowing that it was more than just a one-time thing. It was obvious that Chris had been dating the other chick for quite some time, which explained why he was no longer bothered about his breakup with Lailah.

"You sure you're okay? Talk to me." Zion said in a soft tone. He knew she wasn't being fully honest with him.

"Um, I'll tell you later. I promise." Lailah responded. She wanted to tell Zion what was going on but felt now wasn't the time. She didn't want to ruin their dinner or their time together talking about her ex.

"Aight, I'ma hold you to it." Zion replied. He looked and seen their waiter coming in their direction. They both put in their drink orders and asked for extra time to decide on their entrée. "I got word that both of our birthdays are hella close. And before you came into my life, it was my plan to just drink and go to sleep for my birthday. But I thought we both needed some true alone time." Zion gave Lailah a small white envelope and watched her as she took her time opening it.

"What! St. Lucia?! You never cease to amaze me." Lailah squealed. The anger she harbored about seeing Chris was now a feeling that had been erased.

"Hell yea, I've always wanted to go there. And it would be an honor to go with you." Zion flashed his million-dollar smile.

"Of course. Wait, these tickets are good for a week. Zi! Are you serious?" She exhaled dramatically. " I can't stay out of work that long." Lailah whined.

"Yes, you can. I can pay you for the time you miss. Money is no issue." Zion convinced.

"Well I do have enough PTO time to use up." Lailah stated.

"Good, then it's set." Zion bit his bottom lip.

When their waiter came back to take their orders, they both settled for a 12 oz sirloin steak with a loaded baked potato and veggies. They conversed about their upcoming trip throughout the remainder of their meal. After paying the bill, they drove back to Lailah's apartment. When Lailah put the car in park, she immediately confessed to what had destroyed her mood earlier.

"I seen my ex and his bitch in the restaurant. And the reason why I was so mad is because he was in a whole nother relationship with that hoe while being with me. I thought it was just a one-night stand and shit but nah, clearly it was way more than that." Lailah took a couple hits from the vape pin.

"You still got feelings for this nigga?"

"I did but not anymore. He can choke on bleach twice for all I care." Lailah spat.

There was still some love left from Lailah's end but now,

she felt like Zion was the one to heal her broken heart. Seeing Chris back at the restaurant was the confirmation she needed to move on with Zion. As soon as those words left her mouth, Zion reached over and pulled Lailah in for a kiss. The kiss was short but passionate.

"That's all I needed to know." He stated before they exited the vehicle.

* * *

"Are you sure this is what you want? Are you positive that you're ready for a serious relationship?" Lailah questioned as she and Zion sat in her living room. "My time is too precious for it to be wasted again, and I'm not with the bullshit. Oh, and let me make myself clear, I'm *not* about to share you with anyone else either." Lailah informed him.

Zion wrapped both his arms around her waist and looked deep into her eyes. "Listen, you're the only one who has my attention. I ain't checking for these whack ass hoes out here cause they don't have shit I want. They have nothing to offer. You're the type of female who has all the qualities I want in a wife. You're intelligent, gorgeous, independent, and the list goes on." He paused then stroked her cheek. "I want you all to myself. I want you to be *mine*." Zion was laying out his true feelings.

His confession touched the place in her heart she'd been guarding and shattered the wall she had surrounded it. Lailah went in for another kiss then bit his bottom lip in between. Zion gently pushed her down on the couch. He felt the two of them had reached the next level in their relationship; however, he did not want to assume that meant Lailah was ready to be sexually intimate. He pulled back then stared into her eyes, waiting for her to grant him permission.

"I'm ready." She whispered.

Zion smiled with relief then unzipped her shorts and pulled them down off her legs and threw them to the side. He got on his knees and positioned himself directly in front of her pussy. Zion took off her pink lace panties and tossed them to the floor. He licked his lips before he opened Lailah's legs and gave her pussy a tongue kiss to start off his session. He wasn't surprised at how sweet she tasted because he called it from the start. His tongue was going up and down and around in circles until he found her spot.

"Mmmm. Fuck!" Lailah tried to scoot away but Zion had her legs locked in his grasps.

"Mhmm" Zion moaned. He looked up at Lailah, watching her as she bit her lip to cease her moans. Zion concentrated on her clit and flicked the tip of his tongue over and around her pink pearl. Lailah moved her hips in sync until she felt an explosive orgasm take over.

"Ziiiiiiiiiiii!!! I'm cumminggggggg!!!!" Lailah screamed as her legs started shaking but Zion kept licking, which made her go crazy. Lailah squirted in Zion's mouth, who had a devilish grin plastered on his face. He looked up admiring her as she lay with her eyes closed, trying to catch her breath.

Zion stood then removed his clothing. He watched as Lailah's eyes travelled from his chest down to the place in between his legs.

"Shit." Lailah stated, shocked at the size of his dick. It would be her first time having sex with a man as big as Zion.

"He won't bite." Zion assured.

"He better not." Lailah warned nervously.

Zion kissed her softly as he got on top of her, spread her legs further apart, then placed one of her legs over his shoulder. He could tell she was nervous by the look on her face, so he rubbed the head of his dick up and down her pussy, hoping to help her relax and to see how much wetter she would become.

"Zi, where's your condom?" Lailah questioned.

"This my fucking pussy now. And I wanna feel all of you." Zion said as he stuck the head of his chocolate rod in her opening.

"Shittttt." Lailah moaned, tensing up.

"Relax baby." Zion whispered in her ear. He made slow and steady strokes until she finally listened and loosened up. He kissed her as he dug deep into her tight pussy and was amazed at how good she felt. Zion felt like Lailah's pussy was made of gold as he compared her to all the other females he had sex with. "This my pussy?"

"Fuckkk! Yesssssss!." Lailah screamed.

It took no time for the pain to subside as she began to fuck him back. Zion stopped his stroke and picked Lailah up and carried her to her bedroom. He laid on his back so that Lailah could assume the position on top of him. Lailah took that as her cue; it was her time to show Zion what she was working with and began bouncing up and down on Zion's long shaft like a pro. Zion slapped both her ass cheeks hard, further turning Lailah on. She turned around and gave Zion nothing but ass shots while she grinded deep on his dick. Zion felt himself about to cum but wouldn't let it happen until Lailah got hers first.

"Cum on this dick." Zion instructed. Not one to be outdone, Zion positioned Lailah to lay on her stomach and laid on top of her going deep in her insides.

"Mmmmm!! Shittttt!!Yes, yes, yes! Right there!" Lailah screamed. After a few more strokes, she came hard on his dick as Zion released his seeds inside of her.

"Shit." Zion breathed heavily, slowly pulling out. He turned Lailah over onto her back then kissed her like he had never kissed her before.

Lailah smiled as she reached down and began stroking his long thick log back to life. "Round two?" She asked innocently.

"Round two? Shit that was just the warm up." Zion stated. He eased off the bed then pulled her over to the edge. "Yo ass is in serious trouble now."

CHAPTER 14

The next morning when Zion adjusted his eyes to the morning sunlight, he felt around for Lailah. Looking over to her side of the bed, he discovered she wasn't there. He got up and stepped into the bathroom to wash his face. Inside Lailah's bathroom, he noticed an unopened toothbrush sitting on the sink with a yellow sticky that read: "Use me. ".

"My baby." Zion thought, thinking of Lailah.

He quickly brushed his teeth, washed his face, and stepped out of the bathroom. He found Lailah in her kitchen cooking breakfast; his favorite meal at that. Lailah was in her own world and didn't hear Zion enter the kitchen. When she turned around to place the plate of eggs on the counter, she almost dropped the food when she saw Zion sitting at her table.

"Ughh!! You just couldn't resist could you?" Lailah rolled her eyes. Zion, who was cracking up, went over and gave her a kiss.

"You know I aim to surprise." Zion smacked Lailah's ass and took a seat back at the table. She was wearing a PINK t-shirt and a pair of PINK slippers. It was a breathtaking sight to Zion, who was in awe at how beautiful she was anytime of the day.

"And I'm beginning to learn that. Would you like some jelly or no?" Lailah asked as she set Zion's plate in front of him. She made grits, eggs, sausage, bacon, and biscuits.

"No thank you baby. Who taught *you* how to cook?" Zion questioned. He was particular when it came to his grits. He didn't like them thick or runny, but Lailah had made them just right.

"My mom. I was always curious to learn. When I was eight, I started helping her out in the kitchen." Lailah said as she put butter between her biscuit.

"And how long were you in dance?"

"How'd you know I took up dance?"

"I saw the picture in your living room. You were too cute." Zion commented. He had witnessed that Lailah was even beautiful as a child. He remembered her telling him that growing up, her mother had shown favoritism between her and her sister, making Lailah feel as if she was never good enough. He couldn't understand why her mother would treat her that way or why any parent would for that matter.

"I was only in it for three years until Lauren called herself wanting to do sports. So my mom made me give up dance to satisfy her needs."

"So y'all couldn't do both? Is it because she couldn't afford it?"

"We could, we had the money, but mom never wanted me to outshine Lauren. If there was something I wanted to do and Lauren wanted to do it too, I had to choose something else. Even if I was already in it first."

"That's fucked up."

"Yeah it was. To make up for it, she would buy me clothes, shoes, and toys, but none of those things stopped the hurt."

"What did your father say?"

"Dad was deployed a lot, so he never saw the shit because mom never played favorites when he was around."

"Damn, that's crazy. I don't see how you could treat your kids like that. That shit is fucked up on so many levels. I'm sorry you had to go through that."

"Yea, it eventually came to an end when I finally told my dad what she was doing. It wasn't until I reached middle school when I figured out the name for it. I don't know what my father told her, but she did a whole 180."

"I bet. By the way baby, this food is banging." Zion could hear the hurt in her voice, so he opted to change the subject.

"Thank you love. So what about you? What's on your agenda?" Lailah asked as she took a sip of her orange juice.

"I'ma go and see my mom today. It's time. I been putting it off long enough."

"Why?"

"Because I still hate her with a passion. I know that sounds bad but it's the truth. And I plan on confronting her. The last few times I seen her, I been ignoring my gut feeling and we would have these bullshit ass convos. Fuck alla that. Today, I deserve some answers." Zion replied. There weren't enough words to describe how he felt towards his mom.

"And you have every right to feel the way you do. Let her tell her side and then you tell yours. I know somewhere deep down, you still love her. I can see it in your eyes, it's only covered up with resentment. Try to remain calm during y'all's conversation. Okay?"

"I'll try my best, but I'm not going to make a promise I can't keep." Zion stated then continued to finish his food.

The two of them sat in silence as they finished their breakfast. Once they were done, Lailah grabbed their plates and loaded the dishwasher.

"And wat'chu getting into today?" Zion asked.

"Not a damn thing. Today is my only day off until next week and I'm gonna just chill. I know the bullshit I have waiting for me next week." She answered while wiping the kitchen counter down with a clean dishrag.

"Why won't you quit and let me take care of you?" Zion stated, rising from the table then walking over to her.

"Sounds nice but I need my own money. It's nothing compared to your income, but I'm fine with what I make. I'm not with you for your money and the sooner you realize that, the better off we'll be." Lailah explained. She was slightly annoyed and offended by Zion's offer only because she wasn't after him for what he had. She could care less about the lavish lifestyle he lived.

"I just hate seeing you stressed out. Your bills probably overwhelm you at times, and I don't want you to have to worry about anything. You can move in with me and save money on paying rent." Zion wanted to be around Lailah as much as he could. He was in denial about how quickly he had fallen for her.

"Mmmm, we'll have to see about that." Lailah kissed him on the lips then smiled deviously. "There is something that you can help me with right now." She stated.

"Anything."

"I could really use a nice- warm... shower." She answered suggestively.

"Lead the way."

Lailah took Zion by the hand and led him upstairs to her bathroom. After a round of steamy sex, the two of them finally stepped out and got dressed before exiting Lailah's apartment.

"Thank you for breakfast and dessert." Zion sat on the passenger's side of Lailah's new whip as she drove him home.

"You're welcome."

"I had a great time last night." Zion confessed.

"Me too." Lailah took her eyes off the road for a brief moment. "Can't wait to do it again." She smiled.

"Me either."

" I hope everything goes well with seeing your mom. Let me know when you get there." Lailah stated.

"I hope so too."

CHAPTER 15

*Z*ion's day had started perfectly and he was now hoping his decision to visit his mother wouldn't ruin it. He'd been having second thoughts ever since he got on Highway 74/76 that led to Concord, North Carolina. However, he refused to turn around. He was on his way to a fresh new start in life and he couldn't keep carrying the same baggage. Yo Gotti ft Lil Baby's *Put A Date On It* filled his speakers as he made the three-hour drive. He wanted to smoke a blunt but decided against it. Lailah's advice was the only thing keeping him calm during the whole car ride.

Zion pulled into the visitor's parking lot and turned off his engine. He took a moment before getting out and walking towards the main building. He walked up to the receptionist's desk, who was checking him out, but he made it clear that he wasn't interested. She had a bronze complexion, her red weave was matted towards the ends, she wore big-framed glasses, and had an overbite. Zion still wouldn't have looked her way if he was single. He went towards the elevators and rode up to the fourth floor. Zion walked towards the middle of the hall and knocked on the door. A few moments later, he was greeted by his mother and slowly walked inside.

"Hey baby! It's about time you showed your face. You want something to eat?" Karen offered. It had been almost nine months since she last seen her son.

"Nah, I'm good." Zion declined. "How 'bout we go and sit outside." Zion said.

He provided his mother with one of the best rooms the facility had to offer. Karen's room was set-up like an apartment with modern furnishings. It included a spacious living room, a bedroom with an en suite bathroom, a private balcony, and a fully equipped kitchen.

"Sure. That's fine." Karen replied.

The two of them stepped outside onto the balcony. She took a seat in one of the chairs as Zion sat in the other.

"So how you been feeling?" Zion started the conversation. He chose to play it cool and waited for the right moment to address his true feelings.

"Good. My mind is clearer than it's ever been in years." Karen responded.

I bet it is. Zion thought.

"I've made a couple friends since being here. The staff here is wonderful and very caring. They make the process here a lot easier." She smiled. "What's been going on your end? Anything new?"

"Yea, I met someone. And she's really amazing."

"Whatttttt? I can't believe that. She must be mighty special to take you off the market." Karen knew of her son's bachelor ways along with him being in the game. She knew Zion was paying a pretty penny for her stay and that his funds didn't come from working a nine to five.

"She's more than that actually. Lailah is her name." Zion felt himself getting pissed, he felt his mother was low-key throwing shade. "She makes me want to be a different man...

97

a better one. The love that I been lacking, she fills that hole and then sum." Zion snapped back. He looked at his mother who caught his insult as she adjusted in her seat.

"If you got something on your mind, let it be known." Karen stated.

"You the one throwing jabs. Who are you to call yourself judging someone you don't even know? You got a lot of fuckin' nerve." Zion spat.

"Oh please. You and I know both know you ain't gonna change your ways. For *no* woman. No matter how great she is. So do ya self a favor and stop lying to ya self. Do her a favor and don't lie to her."

"You don't know shit about me! Fuck you mean?" Zion shouted. The nerve of his mother acting as if she knew him personally was beyond Zion.

"I'm your mother."

"Correction, *Claire* is my mother. You only gave birth to me and ain't did shit else since. So what makes you think you deserve that title?" Zion said. He was ready to leave and never come back the way his feelings were set up in that moment.

"What, you just came here to throw shit in my face?! I tried my best!" Karen had tears forming in her eyes. Her heart wasn't ready for this conversation and Zion's comments tore her to pieces.

"You didn't try hard enough. The only thing you cared about was getting high. Not once did you take my well-being and my feelings into consideration. You let that shit destroy you and ruin your life. *And* mine. You were beyond selfish. And I was the one who had to suffer." Zion felt no sympathy for his mom whatsoever. The horrific memories he buried from his childhood came back to flood his mind.

"You ain't no better than me! You sell the shit that kills people!" Karen fumed. She wasn't proud of the choices she made but having to sit there while Zion made her out to be the villain wasn't gone fly in her book.

"Don't try to turn this around on me. What I do is none of your business! All I wanna know is the truth. What or who started you on that shit?" Zion interrogated. He took this as his opportunity to ask the question he'd been waiting to hear his entire life.

"After I had you, it was like everyone had turned their backs on me. No one would help me and your father didn't give a shit about us either. He went on to marry who I thought was my best friend. When I had heard the news, I didn't take it very well."

"So he was the reason?" Zion questioned. There was a part of him that still didn't believe her story.

"He was half the reason. I met this other guy who was about to be signed to the NFL until he injured his shoulder during training camp. His recovery wasn't going so well and he finally gave up hope. He was the one who introduced me to it." Karen revealed. It was hard for her to open that wound, but at the same time, she had to be honest with her son.

"Why couldn't you just say no? Or leave? You coulda stayed with grandma and got a job until you were stable enough to be on your own. Like what the fuck? You let niggas take control over your mind. That's yo problem." Zion had a look of disgust on his face. He couldn't register what his mother was telling him. It was in that moment when he realized that *love* was the worst drug of all time.

"Yea, I'm not afraid to admit that cause I gave your father every piece of me. His no-good ass was playing me the whole entire time! What, I don't have a right to feel the way I do?! Huh?!"

"I'm not saying...."

"Then what are you saying?" Karen cut him off.

"Nothing ma. I'm not saying anything. Yes, he was wrong for what he did. But instead of falling into another man's arms, you shoulda got yo self together first." Zion said in a calm tone. He couldn't blame his mother for how she felt, but he was still bothered by how weak she became for a man. "You let that nigga bring you down to the lowest point in your life. Is that the reason why you never told me about him?"

"That and for other reasons. He left us both and never looked back. But I'm sorry for everything. If I could go back in time and do things differently, I would. I swear." There was an awkward silence between the two of them.

"I accept your apology." Zion finally replied.

He could hear the genuineness in her voice. It wasn't going to happen overnight, but Zion wanted to rebuild the broken relationship he had with his mother. Karen got up from her chair and gave Zion a tight hug as she cried on his shoulder.

"I've been waiting on this moment for a long time." Karen sobbed.

"Me too."

CHAPTER 16

*I*t was after 1 am when Orion entered his one-story home. He felt like he was on top of the world now that things were finally going in his favor. He walked into the kitchen and opened the stove and microwave just to find them both empty.

"So she really didn't cook tonight?" Orion said to himself. "Amber!" Orion yelled but got no response. "Amber, where you at?!" He repeated.

Orion sucked his teeth and proceeded to go to his bedroom when he looked down and stopped in his tracks. There was a trail of blood on his hardwood floors that led to his office. Orion reached in the back of his pants for his strap but froze when he heard a gun being cocked.

"I wouldn't do that if I were you." Zion said as he pressed his Glock 34 to the back of Orion's head. Orion raised both his arms up as his heart began to race.

"What the fuc. . ."

"Shut-up! I ask the mothafuckin' questions." Zion interrupted. A devious smile scrolled across his face as he watched Orion start to sweat. "Where's the safe?" He asked.

"There is no fucking safe!" Orion shouted.

Pop!

"Argghhhhh!!" Orion fell to the floor while holding his knee. He went to retrieve his gun but Zion shot him again in his arm. "Ahhhhh!!" His eyes got wide when he finally seen Zion's face.

"Where's the safe nigga?"

"Fuck you!" Orion yelled.

"You really thought you was gonna get away with taking my shit?" Zion chuckled. "You woulda been better off staying a driver for UPS... you shoulda kept delivering packages bitch. But you wanted to be greedy and grimy. You could never reach up to my level nigga." Zion taunted. "Now I hate that Amber has to be in the middle of this shit, but you brought that upon ya self."

"I swear on everything. . . If you touch her. . . ." Orion started. The pain he was enduring was blocking his threat.

"You ain't gone do *shit*. She a lil tied up right now. And her life is in your hands. You got ten seconds before her ugly-ass becomes maggot food." Zion stated, knowing that Amber was already dead. "10. 9. 8. 7. 6. 5. 4. 3. 2..."

"Alright! Shit!" Orion yelled out. "In the library, push back the shelves." Orion instructed.

Suddenly, five of Zion's goons dressed in all black came rushing in and wearing masks. After taking everything that was hidden in Orion's stash, they left out the back door, each carrying two duffle bags.

"What about my wife?!" Orion pleaded.

"You'll meet her in hell soon."

Pop! Pop! Pop! Pop!

Zion emptied the rest of his clip into Orion's head and walked out feeling no remorse. He walked down the street where he met Derell, who was sitting in his car waiting for him.

"All clear?" Derell asked once Zion got inside.

"Yea. That nigga ain't had no place in this business anyway. He was living comfortably off my work. Shit was pathetic."

"Hell yea. Kyron got the fellas working hard. He says he got a couple prospects that's wanting to join in. I told him I'll let you know so you could fill 'em out for ya self." Derell said.

"Shit getting real out here and these niggas nowadays don't have respect." Zion stated. He needed more workers for the extra product he was about to receive, but his trust was being put to the test.

CHAPTER 17

*L*ailah sat on the edge of her bed as she rubbed lotion up and down her legs. She had just gotten off the phone with her mother, who asked for her to come visit so they could talk. Lailah knew her mother had gotten word about the fight she had with her sister and was in no mood to hear what she had to say. Lailah stepped in her sky-blue sundress and slipped on a pair of sandals. She just wanted to stay in bed after a hard day's work but her mother ruined her plans. Lailah grabbed her keys and headed out the door. As she drove on highway 17, Summer Walker's *Girls Need Love* was played in the background as her mind drifted off to Zion. Lailah found herself falling in love with Zion, which was unlike her because they haven't been together that long. She made a mental note to ask him his true feelings and to see if he felt the same way. Lailah pushed her thoughts to the back of her mind as she prepared for the unexpected once she got to her mother's house. The drive seemed shorter than normal and she was knocking on her mother's door sooner than she anticipated.

"Hey Lailah." Natalie greeted her as she opened the door.

"Hey." Lailah was slightly apprehensive.

"Let's have a seat in the kitchen," Natalie suggested.

Lailah nodded her head in agreement then followed her mother to the kitchen.

"Now I heard what happened between you and Lauren. I'm very disappointed in you. Do you know I had to bail her outta jail?" Natalie said with an attitude.

"Wat'chu getting mad with me for? And you shoulda let that nigga she was whoring with bail her out!" Lailah fumed. It was typical for her mom to take her sister's side in this case, which only infuriated Lailah even more. "But I'm not surprised."

"What are you saying?" Natalie's left eyebrow raised with suspicion.

"I'm think I'm saying it. You can stop pretending with this act you been putting on for years ma. You know your concern is about Lauren and Lauren only. Don't try to play and act as if you care about me. You never did."

"That's a lie! It's nothing but jealousy between you and your sister. And I'm sick of it! Whatever problems you two have, y'all both need to get over it! It's been going on too long." Natalie defended.

"Jealous? Lauren ain't got a pot to piss in! So what makes you think I'm jealous of her?! I'm the one that's doing well, but no, you wanna praise Lauren. And for what? Cause she got a kid that you're taking care of?" Lailah argued. She wanted her mother to admit to her wrongs, and it was now proven that would never happen.

"I don't praise Lauren. I love you both equally. I just want you and your sister to finally get along and stop with the fighting. There's no sense in you both acting like this. It's become old and ridiculous at this point. And I'm over it." Natalie urged. It broke her heart to see her daughters have so much drama between them. She would never reveal that

Lauren was indeed her favorite, who had a hold on her since the day she was born.

"I'm over you lying to protect your image. What is it about her? She's a bum. And yet you have no problem with that. But if it were me, I wouldn't hear the end of it." Lailah stated. She was over giving her mother the benefit of the doubt.

Just when Natalie was about to say something, Lauren came through the door with a huge grin on her face.

"Hey ma." Lauren greeted.

"Hey baby. Where's Heaven?"

Lauren gave her mother a hug and sat down without acknowledging Lailah as if she were invisible. "With her daddy," Lauren answered.

"Mm, that's a first." Lailah blurted.

"Bitch, you got a problem?!" Lauren hissed.

"I already gave you one black eye. Best believe I can give you another." Lailah snapped. She stood up against the table, ready for Lauren to make a move. "Didn't think so." Lailah sat back down when she realized her sister didn't want no smoke.

"Both of y'all... shut-up. Now Lauren, what's your issue with Lailah? Why you keep bashing your sister as if she's some stranger from off the street or something?" Natalie questioned while looking in Lauren's direction.

"She's the one who act like she's better than me! Looking down on me like I'm nothing."

"And you not." Lailah butted in.

"At least my man wants me. Chris was just using yo stupid ass. You just mad cause Riah took him away from you. I make a good ass matchmaker wouldn't you agree?" Lauren smiled as she looked at Lailah's facial expression.

"What are you talking about?" Natalie asked, who was obviously lost.

The next thing Natalie saw was Lailah on top of Lauren, trying to choke her to death. "Stop it!" Natalie screamed. She tried with all her strength to pull Lailah off, but it was no use. Lailah saw nothing but red as she held a handful of Lauren's weave and punched her repeatedly in her nose and face.

"Lailah! Stop it! That's enough! Get off her!" Natalie yelled.

Whap!

Natalie slapped Lailah hard across her face to stop her from beating Lauren any further. Lailah stared at her mother in disbelief.

"Ma..." Lailah whispered.

"That's what you get bitch." Lauren taunted.

"What the hell is wrong with you Lailah? Huh?!" Natalie hollered. She went and got her first aid kit that was in a closet nearby then returned to nurse Lauren's bloody nose.

"Lauren gets off easy once again, I see. Did you not hear what she just said?! Fuck this, I'm out. Don't you call me *ever* again!" Lailah screamed as she stormed out and slammed the door behind her. She got inside her car and drove to Sunset Beach to be alone with her thoughts.

The tears that welled in her eyes raced down her cheeks. This was one of the times where she wished her father was still living. Lailah longed for that father-daughter bond she had been desperately missing.

Buzzz... Buzzz...

Lailah took her phone from out her purse and smiled when she saw Zion calling.

"Hey bae." Lailah greeted.

"What's wrong baby?" Zion immediately heard the sadness in her voice. He paid close attention to her actions and behavioral patterns whenever they would spend time together. Now, he could tell something was bothering her.

"I just had a fight with my sister." Lailah confessed. Her

mind was still racing over what just went down and the nerve of her mother taking up for Lauren once again.

"Where you at?"

"I'm in the parking lot near the beach, getting ready to get out." Lailah said. She used a tissue and wiped away the tears that continued to fall.

"Aight, hold tight. I'm on my way." Zion replied.

"Okay love." Lailah responded as she hung up the call.

She took in a few deep breaths to calm herself as she waited for Zion's arrival. Lailah didn't want Zion to see her looking distraught because she felt as though they haven't reached that level in their relationship. Zion was either speeding or not too far away from where Lailah was because he got there in fifteen minutes. Lailah unlocked her car door and watched Zion as he got in the passenger's seat.

"Tell me what happened." Zion asked as soon as he got in. He pulled Lailah in for a kiss and wiped away the single tear that ran halfway down her cheek.

"My mom called me earlier cause she claimed she wanted to 'talk,' but I knew she was referring to the run-in I had with my sister." Lailah took a short pause in between. "When I got there, she was rambling about some shit I didn't care for, and I again called her out on her shit. But she denied it of course. The shit was a set-up cause in walks my sister a few minutes later and she had a motive also. Me and her exchange a few words and she goes to tell me about her being responsible for hooking up my ex with the girl he cheated on me with. I pounced on top of her, giving her my best shots, and my mom slaps me in the middle of our fight." Lailah held Zion's hand for support as she finished her story. "Her main concern was coming to Lauren's rescue. Not once did she take up for me and put my sister in her place. I've washed my hands with my mother. I can't take it anymore." Lailah expressed.

"You had to do what you had to do. There's no shame in it. You tried your best to get to the root of y'all's issues. She's gonna wish that she took the chance to be honest with you. But I don't want you to feel like you're alone. I'm here for you baby and always will be." Zion kissed the front of Lailah's palm. "You still wanna take a walk?"

"Yea. I wanna get on your back tho." Lailah requested as she got out the car.

She pressed the lock button and placed her keys inside Zion's pocket. She hopped onto Zion's back as he made his way up the stairs on to the sand of the shore. Since it was now nighttime, Lailah didn't have to worry about anyone seeing up her dress. If it was still sunny out, she would have opted to walk alongside Zion. "I'd rather talk about us." She stated.

"I'm all ears baby." Zion said. It felt like he was carrying a light bookbag because Lailah only weighed 140 pounds.

"How you feeling about our relationship so far?"

"I couldn't be any happier. You make me feel things I never felt before. I love being in your presence and when we're apart, I feel incomplete. I feel extremely blessed that you decided to take a chance on a nigga." Zion chuckled.

"Aweee. Me too. And, I'm happy I did. I have no regrets."

"None whatsoever?" Zion sounded like he was shocked. "You've been through so much, and I have too. We both deserve nothing but happiness. And you give me that and so much more. Got me feeling like I'm in a damn Lifetime movie or sum shit." Zion commented. Lailah busted out laughing and kissed him on his neck.

"Stop. Don't start nun." Zion warned. Lailah was messing with one of his spots on purpose.

"Start. . . . What?. . . Hmm?" Lailah said in between kisses. She sucked on his neck, causing him stop in his footsteps.

"Get down," Zion ordered.

He took the blanket he was carrying and spread it along the ground and took a seat with Lailah sitting on top of his lap. There was a fiery spark between them as they gave each other tongue kisses. Zion reached under Lailah's dress and gripped her soft butt cheeks. Lailah unzipped Zion's jeans and brought out his hard dick from his boxers as Zion pushed her panties to the side. Lailah slid down on his thick rod and grinded until she got her rhythm.

"Mmmmm." Lailah moaned in Zion's ear. Her pussy got wetter by the second as Zion moved up and down until he found her g-spot.

"Fuckkk!" Zion groaned. It was like Lailah's hotbox was made just for him. The way she tightened her walls against his dick had him going crazy. "You feel so damn good. Shittt!" Lailah picked up her pace as she wrapped both of her arms around Zion's neck and bounced on his dick. She felt the peak of an orgasm beginning to rise as Zion kept hitting her spot. "Cum for me baby." Zion commanded. He didn't know how much longer he could hold back his nut with the way Lailah was showing out.

"I'm. . . . . . cummmiinnnnnnnnggggg!!!" Lailah yelled out. An electric wave went through her body as her legs gave out. Zion wasn't too far behind her as he kept stroking and spilled his seeds inside her.

"Damn." Zion said as he tried to catch his breath. "What you trynna do to me woman?"

"I'm just trynna love you and be loved back." Lailah answered. She kissed him on the lips as they fixed their clothes and headed back to their cars. "I want some ice cream. You wanna come with me?"

"Of course. I'd rather eat you but I guess I could settle this one time." Zion smiled.

CHAPTER 18

*L*ailah placed her handheld devices on their chargers as she went to the timeclock to swipe her badge. She felt the vibration from her phone and took it out her back pocket to see a text from Janae.

Nae Bug: Best Fran, I know you heard from Liv! I'm throwing a girls night over my place. Come on over! I'm making tacosssssss!!"

Lailah: Aight, let me go home and shower first.

Nae Bug: Girl, cut it out. Zion ass ain't over here, so who you trynna impress? Bring ya ass.

Lailah: Whateva! I'll see yall in a lil bit.

Lailah shook her head at Janae's comment as she took her belongings from her locker and headed out the door. She was excited to see their mutual friend Olivia and to have some girl talk. Lailah popped open her trunk and squealed at the things that were in her sight. Zion bought a brown Michael Kor's bookbag with the matching purse and wallet to go along with it.

"This guy is too much!" Lailah said excitingly. She closed her trunk and got inside her car as she headed to Janae's

apartment. When she made it to the parking lot, Lailah decided to shoot Zion a text.

Lailah: Thank you so much baby! I love my gifts!

Zion: You're welcome my queen. I'm glad you like them and finally found them. Dang, I thought I was gonna have to give you clues and hints.

Lailah: Lmao! I don't use the trunk unless I'm going outta town or something.

Zion: Shit, I see that now. Wyd?

Lailah: I'm at Janae's.

Zion: Okay baby, be safe and call me before you leave.

Lailah: Roger that.

Lailah hopped out her car and knocked on Janae's door. She walked inside and gave their friend Olivia a bear hug. "Look at youuuuu!! I've missed you so much!" Lailah stated.

"I missed you too!" Olivia said. She took a couple steps back and looked at Lailah from head to toe. "I see college been treating you good."

"Girl, not all good. I have so much to catch you up on."

Lailah and Olivia both took a seat at Janae's kitchen table and began fixing themselves a taco salad. Janae joined them as she sat down and handed them both a bottle of water.

"Nah, first we need to know what's going on your end. How's life in the big apple been going?" Janae questioned.

"Well, I don't know where to begin." Olivia shook her head.

"Hell start any where you please." Janae replied. Like Lailah, she was happy to get a surprise visit from Olivia. Olivia became good friends with Janae and Lailah throughout their high school years. She moved away to attend NYU on an academic scholarship to receive her degree in nursing.

"Well, me and Irvin have called it quits."

"What?!" Lailah and Janae said in unison.

"Yep." Olivia confirmed.

"What happened? I thought for sure y'all two were gonna make it." Lailah said in disbelief.

"Girl me too. But niggas will be niggas."

"How'd you find out?" Janae probed.

"I answered his phone while he was in the shower one night. And I asked her who she was and she told me they had been fucking for the last nine months. When he got out the shower, I threw his phone out the window and his clothes."

"I know that's right. But damn Irvin. Nigga's will fuck up a good thing, I tell you." Janae commented.

"Hell yea, always. And then a month after we broke up, I found out I was pregnant."

"Shut-up! Oh my goodness!! Liv!" Lailah covered her mouth in suspense. "How far are you?"

"I'll be eight months in a couple weeks."

"Shit you coulda fooled me, you don't even look no damn eight months. Tell us what you having." Janae asked as she took a sip from the margarita she made.

"A girl." Olivia responded.

"Aweee. I'm happy for you! Have you told him yet?" Lailah questioned as she took a couple bites from her food.

"Nahh, and I don't know when I'ma tell him. I got an interview in Atlanta for this nursing job. I just want to have everything in order before her arrival. You feel me?" Olivia explained. She was glad to receive the support from her friends.

"Well, you know we got'chu if you need help. Don't hesitate to ask. That's what friends are for." Janae gave Olivia a sincere look.

"Thank you guys. How you and Chris doing Lailah?" Olivia said.

"Chris is in the same boat with Irvin, and I just found out that Lauren was the mastermind behind the whole fucking thing. Fuckin' whore." Lailah answered. She patted Janae's back who was coughing as soon as those words left her mouth.

"Nooooooo. She didn't stoop that low Lai." Olivia shook her head.

"Hell yea. I woulda been in jail for attempted murder had not my mother been there."

"And I don't blame you. She's wrong on so many different levels for that. And lemme guess, your mom didn't do shit did she?" Olivia stated.

"Yea, slap me."

"I know you lying." Olivia stated.

"Nope and that was the last straw for me. You wanna give props to your daughter who ain't doing a gotdamn thing with her life and treat me like shit? I don't get it." Lailah ranted. Her heart was still broken over her mother's actions and she didn't know if she could ever forgive her.

"Well one thing I know is a motherfucker will eventually get theirs." Janae stated. "Trust me, those niggas and the family that crossed you will someday need you." She raised her glass.

"I'll toast to that." Lailah agreed.

CHAPTER 19

wo months had passed and Zion had fallen head over hills for Lailah. They had become inseparable since the night he showed up at her spoken word performance. Zion had come to the conclusion that he didn't want to be with anyone else. He wanted Lailah to be his forever. Zion made plans to tell Lailah his true feelings while they were on their getaway, which was in a couple days. Zion was sitting in his car practicing the speech he had made to recite to Lailah. Feeling like he wasn't making any progress, Zion quickly got into work mode and exited his car. When he got inside, he greeted Joel, X, Kel, and Zay, who were all in the kitchen cooking their product and counting money. All four guys had acknowledged Zion and went back to their task at hand. Zion went down the hall and entered an office where he found Kyron sitting on a desk. "How's it been going?" Zion asked. He had built a strong friendship with Kyron and wanted to check in with his personal life.

"Business been going smooth. The family is getting worse tho." Kyron shook his head and ran his hands down his face in frustration.

"Your mom doing okay?"

"Yea, so far so good. She's been home for a couple days now. She just needs a lot of rest." Kyron answered. His mother had recently been diagnosed with breast cancer and had Kyron worrying about her day and night.

"She's definitely a fighter. I'ma keep praying for her."

"Thank you. Lex is pregnant again and the twins are doing okay." Kyron informed him, updating him on his siblings. He was the oldest of his three siblings and had been taking care of them since their mother got sick.

"You gotta be fucking kidding me. You need to go ahead and cut her ass off Ky. I keep telling you man. I understand you wanna help her, but she's only taking advantage of you. Shit has gotten outta hand at this point." Zion ranted. He hated to see his friend get used by his family members because Kyron had a huge heart underneath his tough skin.

"I know man. But who's gonna help take care of her kids?"

"Look, Alexis can get a job. She can put her kids in daycare. All she gives is nothing but excuses. Besides your mom, I can understand you helping your twin sister and brother. But Alexis? It's past time for her ass to do shit for herself instead of having her hand out every chance she gets." Zion stated.

"I'm close to the edge. It's been taking a toll on me." Kyron admitted. He wasn't one to discuss his personal problems but he trusted Zion and his judgment.

"Continue to be strong for your mom. She needs you now more than ever. And don't let your sister become the death of you. Cause the last time I seen you, you looked like shit man. You gotta take care of you first. Let me know if you need anything. Seriously." Zion gave Kyron a brotherly hug because Kyron looked as if he was about to break down at any minute.

"Thanks man. I will." Kyron felt a little weight had been lifted off his shoulders. He was glad to finally release some of the built-up tension he had bottled inside. "So what's been keeping you MIA lately?"

"Welllll. There's a new woman in my life. Lailah is her name." Zion confessed. It brought him a lot of joy to talk about her and to let their relationship be known to others.

"Word? It's serious?" Kyron questioned.

"Yea man. She gone be *wifey*. The crazy thing about it is, we only been dating for about three months. Hell, I didn't know you could catch feelings for someone in that short amount of time."

"Aye, anything is possible. I heard of some couples getting married only one week after being together. But I feel like that's bullshit because ain't no way. But in your case, if it feels real between y'all, you shouldn't question it." Kyron said. He was very mature for a guy his age and his mother played a huge part in helping him become the man he was.

"And I don't. She changed me in so many ways. I don't see no one but her."

"I'm happy for you. You deserve true love cause I know yo ass was getting tired of those fake bitches you were used to entertaining." Kyron laughed.

"Hell yea. Shit get old after a while. You been talking to anyone new?"

"Don't have the time. Whoever she is, we'll eventually cross paths. I fa sho ain't rushing shit." Kyron had his heartbroken a year prior when he found out he wasn't the father to a son from his girlfriend of three years. The results turned his heart black and cold, inciting him to give up on love.

"Feel you on that. Keep ya head up." Zion knew of Kyron's past love life and his heart went out to him. He commended Kyron for being the bigger person and walking away in the situation. Any other time, Kyron would've put a bullet into his ex, Naomi, but he was working on his anger and maturity at the time. It was a hard decision but he ultimately decided to let her live. Kyron grew up without a true mother figure in his life and he didn't want Naomi's son to endure the same kind of pain.

"I can handle the extra shipment you got coming in. I need the money." Kyron urged. He was tired from working long hours, but he was saving up his money to buy businesses as well. It wasn't his plans to keep hustling forever, which was something he had yet discussed with Zion.

"You positive? What happened to the guys you had lined up?" Zion was curious at Kyron's sudden need for extra weight, but he didn't question it.

"Something wasn't sitting right with me. So I did a deeper investigation and they turned out to be some snake ass niggas."

"Figures. But aight, I'll keep you updated. Continue to keep ya eyes open." Zion instructed.

"Cool. Yo ass is hitting on thirty's door and shit. What's ya plans?"

"Tell me why me and my girl's birthdays are a day apart? But I'm taking her to the Caribbean… she's never been on a real vacation before. So this should be interesting." Zion smiled. He was more than excited to be away from any distractions and to have some alone time with Lailah.

"I hope y'all enjoy yourselves. You been working hard these past eight months, you need some time off."

"Exactly and just a few more months and I'll be ready to hang this shit up." Zion didn't know who he would choose next to take over his throne. Both Kyron and Derell had the qualities and mindset to run his empire. It would be one of the hardest decisions yet for Zion to make. Zion and Kyron walked back towards the kitchen and seen the four men packaging up the coke and putting rubber bands around the stacks of money.

"What's the count?" Zion asked as he walked in their direction.

"2.5 mill." Kel answered as Zion nodded his head. Zion then gave each guy some dap and gave off his instructions before making his exit. Zion left out the door feeling like the king himself.

He headed over to Derell's private community, which was located in Leland, NC. He pulled into the driveway of Derell's dark brick one story home. Zion hopped out his car and ringed the doorbell. A few seconds later, he was greeted by Derell, who was holding a bag of Doritos in his hand.

"Wassup?" Zion walked inside and followed Derell to his kitchen.

"Shit, you got good timing. I'm in the middle of making burgers, you want one?"

"Yea, but don't put no damn cheese on mine. I know how you is." Zion said, taking a seat at the bar.

"Hating ass. Anyway, you met up with the fellas?"

"That's where I'm coming from now. Final count checked out, so I couldn't ask for nothing more." Zion confirmed. There was never a time when his money came up short throughout his time being at the top of the game.

"Shit, that's always good. You packed and shit for y'all's trip?"

"Almost. Tell ya the truth, my ass a lil nervous. I just want everything to be perfect."

"Aye, don't sweat it. Just be you and everything else will fall into place." Derell knew what Zion was referring to and it was a sight to see him worked up over a woman.

"I'll try. You still kicking it with Janae?"

"Yep. She's starting to grow on a nigga. A little bit more." Derell said as he flipped their burgers in the pan.

He then took out the fries that were done and placed them onto separate plates. Derell went to his refrigerator and took out some condiments to put on their burgers and a couple of beers.

"Ahhh shitttt." Zion chuckled as he accepted his Corona from Derell.

"Forreal tho. I never thought I'd be the one saying this, but I'm really feeling her. The only thing that's standing in the way is her job situation. Her relying on her parents ain't cutting it with me. She needs to learn how to be on her own without her parents' money." Derell vented. Janae's bratty attitude was a little annoying to Derell at first, but now it became sad in his eyes.

"Maybe that's where you come in and help her." Zion commented. He took his plate from Derell and placed mustard and mayo on his bun and put it back on top of his burger. He took a couple bites as he closed his eyes and savored the flavor. Derell was a good cook whenever he chose to be.

"Damn, is it good?" Derell noticed Zion's facial expression, who hadn't said a word since he started eating.

"Shut-up nigga. And yea, it's aight." Zion played it off.

"The fuck it is. But back to the conversation, I don't think I have the patience for that. She whines over lil shit and I'm not used to alla that."

"And I'm pretty sure there are some things about you that she isn't used to either. You gotta take that into consideration. Y'all both gonna have some traits that are gonna irritate the other. You gotta look past that shit." Zion preached. "There are a couple things that aggravate me with Lai but her pros outweigh her cons in the end."

"Really?"

"Yea nigga. I'm not saying our relationship is peaches and cream all the time. No relationship is. It's just you must compromise in a relationship. And if you really digging Janae, you should give it a shot. You neva know. She's prolly what yo ass need." Zion stated as he dipped a couple of his fries in some ranch dressing.

"I don't know if she's worth the headache. If I drop Simone and Maria, they might not never come back."

"And that's one of yo problems right there. Fuck them. Yo main concern is pussy. Let them hoes go." Zion spat. "But take me and Lailah for example."

"That's completely different. Lailah has a job and pays her own bills. You can't compare her to Janae." Derell argued.

"You missing the point. Yea that's true but I was still afraid to get with her because I didn't want to end up wasting my time. With her being a school girl and all, I thought she was gonna be boring or sum shit. But the more time I spent with her, she turned out to be real cool, and now I can't get enough of her."

"Mhmm. I still have my doubts man. It's a huge risk I'll be taking. And I don't wanna end up jinxing shit with me and her." Derell took a swig from his beer. "How yo visit go with ma dukes?"

"At first we was going back and forth with each other but in the end, she apologized. So now we're going to work towards repairing our relationship. Baby steps."

"Your mom young tho, right?"

"Yea, she had me when she was 19. Turns out, my dad was the main cause for her addiction. He left her high and dry for her best friend and went and made a new fucking family." Zion spat. There weren't enough words to explain Zion's hate for his father after hearing what went down between his parents.

"Damn, that's deep."

"Hell yea, which is why I could see her point of view

because before, I really wasn't trynna hear shit. But I still felt like she shouldn't have given up that easy."

"And you right. But I guess when you young and in love, shit can obviously screw you up. She didn't know how to rebound from him." Derell was happy that Zion could hash things out with his mother because it's been a long time coming. "Did she tell you anything else about him?"

"Yea and I plan on visiting that nigga too."

"Where he living now?"

"In Raleigh, so not far at all."

"Do you wanna give him another chance or. . ."

"FUCK no!" Zion cut Derell off before he could finish his sentence. "That nigga didn't care about my life. He made that clear when he walked away and never looked back. He basically said 'fuck me,' and I can't respect a dude like that."

"I don't understand how any parent can neglect or abandon their kids. That's fucked up. And it says a lot about that person and their character." Derell shook his head and finished his food. Derell's mother had died shortly after giving birth to him, and his father was a dead beat who constantly came in and out of his life. Derell ended up being raised by his mother's older sister.

"It was his decision to leave and also the wrong the one." Zion replied.

CHAPTER 20

Zion took Lailah by the hand as he helped her down the steps off his private jet. They walked hand in hand towards Zion's Escalade Yukon as their driver chauffeured them inside and drove towards their living quarters. Zion held Lailah's hand and sat back as he watched her check out the scenery of the island.

"Babeeeee! This place is beautiful!" Lailah exclaimed.

"I'm glad you approve. I wouldn't wanna share this experience with anyone else but you." Zion kissed Lailah on the lips as he invited her tongue inside his mouth.

When they pulled up to their gated penthouse, Lailah was at loss for words. Zion chuckled at her reaction as he tipped the driver and hauled their luggage inside. He went and hugged Lailah from behind as she gazed at the ocean view.

"Let's take a tour." Zion recommended.

Their villa was private and secluded that gave them tons of privacy for obvious reasons. It was furnished and decorated with ultra-modern touches. They had a chef-styled all white kitchen with double ovens and a large island. The living room was spacious with white plush couches with glass sliding doors that presented a wide-view of the ocean. They had a covered deck with a built-in infinity pool and steps that led to direct access to the beach. The master bedroom had a king-sized canopy bed with white drapes and en suite bathroom that consisted of a clawfoot tub, a glass walk-in shower with rain showerheads and separate counter spaces. A 50" inch television rested on the wall of their bedroom and living room. The villa came with 24 hour dine-in specials with access to clubs and restaurants. There was a personal chef and housekeeping on stand-by as well. Zion made sure to spare no expense for Lailah and to have her not wanting for anything.

"I'm in need of a shower. Care to join me?" Lailah said as she got undressed and went inside the bathroom.

"I'm right behind you." Zion replied. When he took off his shirt, revealing his rock-hard abs, Zion smiled when he seen Lailah fanning herself.

"Bring that sexy ass chocolate this way." Lailah motioned with her index finger. She turned on the shower and adjusted the temperature to both their liking. She stepped inside with Zion following right behind her.

"Thank you." Lailah stated.

"For what?"

"For everything." Lailah answered. She put her hands around Zion's neck as they kissed each other passionately while the water rained down on both their bodies. The warmness from the water only intensified their moment as Zion picked Lailah up and placed her against the wall. Lailah fumbled for a few seconds until she grabbed what she had been wanting and stuffed Zion's dick inside her tight tunnel.

"Ahhhh!" Zion and Lailah both cried out at the same time. Zion stayed locked in that position to embrace the wonderful feeling that was present between them. He began to slowly slide in and out of Lailah while looking into her eyes. He spread her legs further apart to give her deeper penetration, which made her go wild.

"Yesssss!!! Yessssss!!!" Lailah moaned out. The position Zion had her in only made it easier for him to hit her special spot.

"Feel that shit? Huh?" Zion groaned in her ear. The feeling Lailah's pussy gave him was out of this world. He had rawed a couple other girls in his lifetime but none of them compared to Lailah. Not one girl from his past topped Lailah's performance when it came to sex. It was as if their bodies had been designed specifically for each other.

"Yesss!! Baby Yess!! Shittttttttt!!!" Lailah screamed as she held on tighter to Zion's neck. She was ready to explode at any second as she tried to hold back.

"Stop fighting it and let go! Let that shit go!"

"Fuckkk! Ziiiiiiiiii!!!" Lailah released her juices down Zion's dick.

"Ahhhhhh!" Zion then shot his load up Lailah's love tunnel.

"I love you!" Lailah whispered.

"I love you too."

CHAPTER 21

*L*ailah looked up at the stars in the sky as Zion held her from behind. It was their last night in paradise of their eight-day trip. During their time on the island, Lailah and Zion participated in various activities. They took interests in snorkeling, horseback riding, ziplining, going on a cruise, dancing, and shopping. Lailah was overcome by many emotions when their stay had come to an end. St. Lucia became one of her favorite places to visit and vacation.

"I hate to leave this place." Lailah's voice dripped with sadness. She was thankful that they took a lot of pictures to start a collection. Zion wasn't a huge fan of taking photos but for Lailah, he'd proven to do anything for her.

"We can stay another week. Two weeks. Whenever you wanna come back, just let me know." Zion bent down and kissed Lailah on her neck. The light perfume she was wearing danced around his nostrils and made his dick hard as a brick.

"You really mean that?"

"Of course baby. Making you happy and keeping you happy are my top priorities. Shit, I don't wanna leave eitha."

Zion confessed. He stood back as Lailah turned around to face him.

"I have a question. And I want you to be completely honest with me. I won't get mad or anything if you say no but just don't lie to me. But I wanna know. . ."

"Yes, I'm in love with you." Zion finished her sentence. He couldn't believe that he finally said the words he been hiding all along, but he was happy to get it off his chest. It was tearing him apart inside to keep his true feelings hidden.

"But are you sure? I can't put myself out there or my heart just to get hurt again. My heart can't take another loss." Lailah explained. She was afraid to love again but being with Zion made her feel safe and that she had nothing to worry about.

"Yes baby, I'm sure. I know I've never been in love before, but what I feel for you runs hella deep. To my soul deep. Since the day we met at your job, you were mine. I just didn't know it yet. You bring so much joy into my life and I can't imagine you not being in it." Zion kissed Lailah on her lips, pulling her close. "I love you so much. More than anything in this world."

"I love you too." Lailah held Zion's hand as he led her back to their place. Zion had their chef prepare them dinner for their last night and had a romantic set-up on their private deck. There were candles and rose petals leading up to their table where there was champagne, strawberries, chocolate and whip cream sitting on a separate table. Zion held out Lailah's chair and scooted her to the table. He sat down and flashed his pearly whites as their chef appeared and sat down two silver platters in front of them. When their cook took the tops of their meals, Lailah's eyes glistened at her meal.

"Zi, this is beautiful. And this food looks amazing." Lailah looked over the stuffed spinach salmon with white potatoes and broccoli. The waves in the background and the cool breezes added on to their private moment.

"I had to make our last night special. And I agree, this looks delicious." Zion dismissed their chef and began to cut up his salmon.

"You outdid yourself with this whole trip. Too bad we gotta face reality tomorrow. I need to go school shopping too. New jeans are calling my name."

"When do you start back?"

"Two weeks." Lailah sighed and rolled her eyes. She was beyond ready to graduate and be done with school. It was only wishful thinking because she had another three years to go before she would be done with graduate school.

"I know you tired of it baby. Hell, I'm tired for you. But you're almost to the finish line. I admire your strength, tolerance, and drive. How well you handle being under pressure from your heavy workload. You amaze me in a way I can't explain." Zion stated. He meant every word he said and wondered to himself how he was so lucky to have Lailah in his life.

"If it wasn't for God's grace and mercy, I don't know how I would've done it." Lailah replied. "Plus bud helps out as well. A lot a lot." Lailah chuckled.

"I bet. So I take it you're not much of a drinker. Because you didn't take many shots that night at the club. And here now, you only took a few sips of the bubbly."

"Nahhh, I'll leave that to you and Janae. I been drunk a couple times before and I hated the way it made me feel. I prolly didn't do it right, but I don't give a fuck. I'll stick to smoking and that's it." Lailah clarified. She hated drinking and would only take a shot to please her best friend.

"Well it ain't for everybody." Zion agreed. "Have you decided on where you wanna go for graduate school?"

"Ummm. I was leaning towards going to Atlanta. How you feel about moving your business over there?"

"Atlanta huh? Well I'll be straight by then, so it won't be no problem. North Carolina is starting to get on my nerves anyway."

"Really? How so?"

"Mainly, their laws. Can't do shit out here," Zion shook his head and downed his glass of champagne.

"Hell yea. But I haven't made up my mind yet. It was just a thought. You and Janae will be the first ones to know my decision."

"All I ask is you just keep me in the loop. But I have a few other things I need to get off my chest." Zion took another bite from his salmon before continuing. He looked at the scared expression on Lailah's face and said "Chill, baby. It's nun but good things." Zion smiled. "I just want you to know that I can't see myself without you. You make me a better man in ways I didn't know was possible. Before you came into my life, I was lost and was close to giving up hope for love. You're the first and only female who caught my attention to where it's more than just sex for me. The connection we have is more than that, because I see a future with you. Which lets me know that I'm in love. All I think about is you. All day long. You truly make me happy." Zion wasn't one to get emotional and Lailah was the one who helped bring out his soft side. "So are you ready to make our love last?"

"More than anything." Lailah answered. She watched Zion stand up and take out a black velvet box. "Zi? What are you. . . What are you doing?" Lailah now had tears streaming down her face as Zion bent down on one knee.

"Lailah Camille Henson. Will you marry me?" Zion asked. He opened the box that revealed an eight-carat cushion-cut diamond ring with a pave diamond platinum band.

"Yes!!!!"

CHAPTER 22

*L*ailah was under her covers texting Zion, smiling and laughing at the conversation they were having. It had been a few days since they been back in the United States. Zion tried once again to persuade Lailah to move in with him but she declined. Lailah was so used to having her own place and privacy that she was dreading her new living arrangements. It'd be a huge change living with a man and she was still trying to mentally prepare. Lailah's thoughts were interrupted when she got an incoming call from her friend Olivia.

"Hey Liv! What's going on wit'cha?" Lailah answered on the first ring.

"Nothing girl, are you busy today?"

"Nah, I'm just here chilling. Why, wassup?"

"I was wondering if I could come over and talk to you."

"Yea, that's no problem. How far away are you?"

"Well I'm in Supply right now. So it'll be another forty minutes before I make it."

"Ok, cool. Well I'ma get ready and call me when you get close."

"Okay girly. Bye."

"Bye." Lailah hung up and rushed to her bathroom. She had been off from work for two hours and didn't mind entertaining for the rest of the evening.

Once Lailah got out the shower, she brushed her hair into a ponytail and put on a pair of black leggings with a PINK t-shirt and PINK bedroom slippers to match. As if on cue, Lailah grabbed her phone and went to the door to greet Olivia.

"Hey girl. Are you sure you're almost eight months?" Lailah commented as she gave her friend a warm hug. She looked at Olivia up and down and was amazed at how her baby bump was barely noticeable.

"Yes girl. I may not look it but I fo damn sho feel it." Olivia giggled. The bond she shared with Lailah was different than the one she had with Janae. Lailah was more understanding and wasn't quick to judge whereas Janae was too self-centered at times.

"Take a load off and make yourself comfortable. Would you like something to drink?"

"Water please."

"Coming right up." Lailah took a cold bottle of water from her refrigerator and went to take a seat next to Olivia. She handed Olivia her bottle and noticed the uneasiness in eyes. "So tell me about this job you got lined up."

"Well the position that I applied for was to work in the Intensive Care Unit. They would start you off with 16 an hour."

"Shitttt. You'll get it, I'm sure. I'll be sure to pray for you and baby girl."

"Thank you. So I finally told Irvin and he says he's gonna be there, but I ain't gonna hold my breath on it. Ion need his ass for shit, and I don't believe anything he says. So I'm not gonna stress over it. He's the one gonna be missing out, not me" Olivia seethed. She felt all types of ways about being a single mother. She understood she wasn't the first and wouldn't be the last.

"Exactly. The fuck-nigga population is only getting higher. Sad to say." Lailah agreed.

"Niggas couldn't last an hour in our shoes."

"Preach."

"When they get sick, they act like punk-ass bitches. Man the fuck up! Shit. So I know they couldn't take having periods. They wouldn't know what the fuck to do then." Olivia joined in with Lailah, who was close to falling off the couch from laughing so hard. They both gave each other a high five as they caught their breaths.

"Their mindset is all the way fucked up. I don't understand their stupid ways of thinking. They expect us to just be okay and forgive them when they fuck up or cheat, but let us do that shit and it's War World 3. I don't get it." Lailah chimed in. She completely understood where Olivia was coming from.

"Talk to me." Olivia said. With the hormones she was experiencing, she was glad to be back in the presence of her friend. They hadn't seen each other in two years but kept in contact over Facetime and texting. Lailah knew the right things to say to make Olivia worry less and to feel at ease. "They a trip, I tell you. Have you decided on a name yet?"

"Yes. Mia Ry'elle Matthews." Olivia responded.

"I love that, her ass gonna be spoiled rotten. Three times over. Between you, your mom, and me."

"She's already spoiled. My mama done bought so much stuff, it's unbelievable. I don't think I'ma need a baby shower."

"You betta have one. And stop playing."

"I will. I'm just. . . Bitchhhhhhh!!! I can't believe I'm just now seeing this!" Olivia yelled, looking at Lailah's engagement ring. "Oh my damn! Congratulationsssssss!!! Oh my goodness!!! Why didn't you tell me?! I'm sitting here rambling and shit." Olivia examined Lailah's ring and was in awe.

"I was trynna see how long it would take you." Lailah stated.

"Oohhhweeeeee!! Who is this mystery man? He did a damn good job! Cause that rock is sum serious!"

"His name is Zion." Lailah went through her phone and showed Olivia a picture they took together.

"Nice catch girl. Y'all a good-looking couple." Olivia commented. Lailah had a special glow to her that Olivia had never seen. One she didn't have whenever she was with her ex Chris.

"We just got back from our vacation in St. Lucia."

"St. Lucia?! Oh, I know this nigga got some dough. What he do? Cause Chris broke ass couldn't afford to take y'all nowhere."

"You ain't gonna believe it. But guess."

"He a lawyer? Doctor? Surgeon? Professor? Professional player?" Olivia questioned. "I give up. Tell me." Olivia said as Lailah shook her no to all her guesses.

"Drug dealer." Lailah blurted.

"Lailah, stop lying and tell me forreal."

"I'm serious."

"That's hard for me to believe. Outta all the people? You?"

"I know, I know. I'm shocked at myself too. He has everything I ever wanted in a man. He puts up a hard shell for his business of course, but underneath all that, he lets me see his sensitive side. I'm the first woman that he chose to take a chance with."

"So he's never been in a relationship before?"

"Yea."

"That raises a red flag." Olivia stated honestly.

"Trust me, he's the truth."

"He better be." Olivia warned. "And as long as your happy, I'm happy. I can see he been treating you good. Have you guys set a date yet?"

"Yes, October 18th."

"Damn! Why so quick?"

"Well he didn't wanna wait too much longer and wanted to have the wedding before this year was over with. And you know I don't do the cold weather either, so I opted for the fall. Plus it's gonna be a very small and private ceremony. I was thinking about you as well because you would have Mia by then. It's only gonna be you and Janae and Zion's close friends slash partners."

"You not inviting your mom?" Olivia asked.

"Hell no. She's cut off."

"Understandable. What venue have you selected?" Olivia felt her baby kicking and rubbed her belly.

"Back in St. Lucia"

"I'm excited for you. You deserve nothing but the best."

"Thanks Liv."

"Geez." Olivia rubbed her stomach.

"What's wrong?" Lailah asked, immediately concerned.

"Mia be throwing those blows." She took a deep breath then exhaled. "You wanna feel her kick?"

"Of course." Lailah smiled. Olivia took Lailah's hand and pressed her palm against the left side of her belly. "Aweeee! I can't wait for that moment." Lailah gleamed.

"You'll have it soon enough." Olivia predicted.

Olivia filled Lailah in on her time in New York and what's life been for her since she moved. An hour went past and Lailah walked Olivia to her car and gave her a warm hug.

Olivia would be making the trip to Georgia in the next couple of days and was informed by Lailah that she could be possibly moving out there as well. The thought of having her good friend in the same state made Olivia ecstatic. Lailah gave Olivia one more hug then watched her drive off.

CHAPTER 23

*A*fter seeing Olivia off, Lailah went back inside and changed into a vertical striped cami romper and white sandals. She gelled her hair into two flat twists and headed out the door to meet Janae. When she got to the parking lot in Olive Garden, she quickly found a space and walked inside. Lailah followed the hostess that led her to the booth where Janae was sitting.

"Glad to finally see you!" Janae stated, giving Lailah a quick hug.

"I know right. As soon as I came back, work was there waiting on my ass." Lailah chuckled. She couldn't deny that she missed Janae's free-spirited personality.

"No he didn't!!! Lailahhhhhhh!!!" Janae noticed the big rock on Lailah's ring finger and was taken back. Her eyes got big as she lifted Lailah's hand up for a closer view. "Details! Details!" Janae squealed, clapping her hands. "Wait wait wait. Before you tell me. How was the trip?"

"Girl, it was like a dream. The layout of the home was fantastic. We had 360 ocean views, personal cook, the whole nine. My ass even went swimming and you know I hate going under water." Lailah commented. She gave their wait-ress her drink order and decided on an appetizer as well. Their conversation resumed once their orders had been put in. "But girl, he proposed on the last night and it was sooooooo romantic."

"Y'all set a date?"

"Mhmm. October 18th."

"Y'all both in a rush or sum?"

"Nahh. Well I guess he was. But I didn't wanna wait too much longer either. How you and Derell?

"We good. He just keeping throwing hints that he wants more than just fucking. But it's like I don't wanna take it there to get disappointed by his answers. Ya know?"

"I feel you. But y'all need to have a conversation about it tho. You don't need any mixed signals whatsoever to make things more complicated. Fuck that. Talk to his ass and see where he stands."

"Yea, you're right. His immaturity gets on my fucking nerves, which is why I can never take him serious." Janae vented. She didn't know if it was really lust or real feelings starting to develop. It was easy and common for her to confuse the two.

"Maturity is the main thing that niggas lack and it's a fucking disgrace. But he's gonna have to step up and put that whoring shit to rest. Life is more than just getting pussy." Lailah said in a disgusted tone. She knew firsthand what it was like to date a dude who still acted as if he was still a teenager.

"He's gonna have to do more than that." Janae added and took a brief pause. "Because he's about to become a daddy."

"Oh shit…" Lailah blurted in disbelief.

CHAPTER 24

"**G**ood morning," Zion said as Lailah looked up from her pillow. He had been watching her sleep for the last twenty minutes after discussing business with a potential investor. Now that Lailah had agreed to become his wife, Zion wanted nothing more than to get the rest of his affairs in order to finally leave the game for good.

"Morninggggg," Lailah yawned. She scooted over towards Zion and rested her head on his chest.

"How'd you sleep?"

"Like a baby." Lailah smiled as she reached down inside his boxers and slowly stroked his large manhood.

"You gonna be the one to make us late." Zion bit his lip. He loved Lailah's touch when she freely gave him hand jobs. Her grip was firm and soft at the same time, and she knew how to work her magic.

"Yea, you right. I'm trynna beat the afternoon rush." Lailah replied. Zion was taking Lailah shopping for whatever she needed for school and personally. As much as Lailah tried to reject Zion's offer, his persistence ended up winning the battle. "C'mon here, cause you take longer to get ready than me sometimes." Lailah stated.

"You know you like yo man fresh." Zion responded as they slid out of bed.

"Damn sure do."

After taking a shower, Lailah went into her own personal closet that Zion had set up for her a couple weeks prior. It was a wrap-around closet that held her purses, clothes and shoes in separate spaces. Lailah chose to wear light denim high-waisted shorts, a white cami that exposed her breasts, and red converses. Her spiral curls were visible from the quick wash-n-go she performed, and she picked up a pair of Ray ban sunglasses that were positioned next to her jewelry. Lailah walked behind Zion towards his garage and stopped in front of one of his luxury cars.

"Can we take this one for today?" Lailah pointed at the black Mercedes C-class Benz.

"Sure," Zion went back inside and retrieved the keys and handed them over to Lailah. He got inside the passenger's seat and looked at Lailah who was smiling from ear to ear.

"When's the last time you drove this car?" Lailah asked as she slowly backed out of the driveway. She was in heaven and felt like the car was floating by how smooth it drove. Zion passed over a blunt he just finished rolling and turned up the volume to Avant's *Read Your Mind* that was playing from his music list.

"It's been almost a month now. I only drive this car and my Range Rover for special occasions. Like right now for example." Being the bigtime kingpin he was, Zion always kept a low profile for many reasons. He couldn't afford any mishaps or anything that could put his position in jeopardy.

"Lemme ask you something. Do you think or believe that Derell is ready to commit?"

"No. He just needs some more time to figure out what he

wants to do with his love life. Why you ask?" Zion didn't know what Lailah intent was but was eager to find out. It was their first time having a conversation about his friend and Zion didn't know what to think of it.

"Because Janae wants to know where they stand. Yo fran is giving off different signals and shit. That shit ain't cool. I just don't wanna see my best friend get hurt. You could understand that." Lailah defended.

"Yes, I see where you coming from. I already said my peace and advice to Derell. And right now, he's just letting everything I told him marinate in his mind. I believe he's gonna do the right thing. I wouldn't let him come at yo friend any type of way." Zion said calmly. Truthfully, he didn't know whether or not his words did any good. Sometimes talking to Derell was like talking to a brick wall.

"Okay." Lailah replied. She had a slight attitude and remained quiet for the next ten minutes.

"Have you picked out a dress yet?" Zion directed their conversation to a more positive topic. He wanted to avoid any conflict or arguments that was close to appearing.

"I'm still torn in between these four different styles. They have to be just right, even though I'm only gonna be wearing it for a couple hours." Lailah took the half of blunt from Zion and took a couple long pulls. They had made the two-hour drive to Raleigh, where Lailah pulled into the parking lot of Crabtree Valley Mall. After she found a space, they walked in the mall hand in hand.

CHAPTER 25

*Z*ion bought clothes for Lailah from American Eagle, Aerie, Banana Republic, Forever 21, H&M, Pacsun, Victoria's Secret, and PINK. By the time they were finished with their shopping spree, Lailah and Zion's hands were both filled with numerous bags. Zion had a fun time shopping with Lailah because he got to experience a free fashion show, featuring Lailah modeling different types of jeans and lingerie and because he loved seeing her smile.

"Where you wanna eat?" Zion asked. He volunteered to drive when Lailah had mentioned she was getting tired. It was still early in the afternoon, so Zion decided to head back to their hometown.

"Let's go to Bone Fish Grill. Call or text your friend Derell and I'll invite Janae."

"Why can't it just be us?"

"I mean, why not? I haven't been on a double date in forever, so why not have some people we know to accompany us?" Lailah stated. There was an underlying motive she had, but it wasn't for Zion to know.

"Okay." Zion reluctantly agreed. This deep into their relationship, Zion could tell when Lailah was up to something. He had to remain patient in order to figure out what it was.

As Lailah relaxed in the passenger's seat catching a nap, Zion's mind wondered off to their future ceremony. At first, he wanted a huge wedding with all the extras that came along with it. After talking out the details with Lailah, he agreed that it would be best for them to have a small and private wedding. Zion had a lot of enemies that were lurking in the shadows to take over his status, so he had to remain low-key even with his love life. If something were to happen to Lailah because of him, he wouldn't know how to live with himself. Zion pulled into the congested parking lot of the restaurant. He lightly shook Lailah out of her sleeping somber and kissed her palm.

"You must've been dreaming of something good, cause yo ass was snoring up sum. How could sum so little make such a loud noise?" Zion chuckled.

"Oh hush. Yo ass ain't got no room to talk. I'm just catching up on the sleep my ass lost this past week." Lailah playfully shoved Zion.

When she spotted Janae, she wasted no time getting out the car and meeting her. Zion got a knock on his window and looked to see a puzzled expression on Derell's face.

"Why she here?" Derell asked, referring to Janae.

"Lailah wanted to invite her, so. Are y'all two on bad terms or sum?"

"Nah, we just haven't talked in a couple days."

"Well, there should be no problems then. We just came here to eat and have good conversation." Zion assured.

"Fine with me."

"How's Jalen been doing?"

"Real good actually. He been pulling in twice as more than he used to. Your tactics scared the fuck outta him."

"It's the only way you learn," Zion said. He seen both the girls walking in their direction as he opened the door then exited the vehicle. He noticed that Derell and Janae hadn't said two words to each other as the four of them proceeded inside the restaurant. *Something ain't right.* He thought. He pushed the thoughts out of his head then said a silent prayer, hoping things would go smoothly. Inside the restaurant, they were all seated to a table as Zion once again noticed the awkwardness between Janae and Derell. Their waiter appeared and took their drinks and appetizer orders and left as quickly as he came.

"So how's the wedding planning coming along?" Derell asked Lailah.

"Good. Coral is going to be the color. We have the venue and reception already booked. So all the big important things have been taken care of. All we have left to do is you guys' tuxes and our dresses." Lailah answered.

"Which is a challenge within itself." Zion added. He handed Lailah her glass of water and gave their waiter their entrees orders. Everyone dug into their appetizers as Lailah saw Derell give Janae a salty expression.

"What's the matter?" Lailah looked in Derell's direction.

"What you mean?" Derell asked but knew what she was talking about.

"If you wanna act like a dumbass, then that's on you. But what's your issue with Janae? You acting like you can't stand to be around her right now or sum."

"There is no issue. Don't speak on sum you know nothing about." Derell shot back. He turned and saw the scowl on Janae's face and was ready to get up and leave.

"Aye, what's your problem?" Zion looked at Lailah who ignored his question.

"I know enough. If you don't wanna be in a relationship with Janae, then tell her. If all you want is sex, tell her. Stop giving her the runaround. Y'all niggas kill me. Y'all wanna have y'all cake and eat the shit too. And I'm here to tell you that you got life fucked up thinking that's the way it supposed to go." Lailah seethed. She was tired of Derell's bullshit and felt the need to call him out.

"Zion get ya fiancée brah."

"Only I control me. Not Zion." Lailah corrected.

"I don't know what's going on, but I think both of y'all need to calm down." Zion looked from Lailah to Derell. It was obvious Lailah felt some kind of way towards his partner, but she had chosen the wrong place to address the issue.

"Is this how you feel too? Or you gonna let your friend fight ya battles." Derell asked Janae. He felt somewhat embarrassed the way Lailah came for his character.

"Yea I'm tired of you putting up this front but behind closed doors, you wanna be in my ear telling me sum different. And I wanna know right here and right fuckin' now. What do you want?" Janae said, giving Derell a sad look. She was tired of the back forth between her and Derell and the suspense was beginning to kill her.

"I thought about it and if you want my official answer in front of everybody.... it's no. I thought I was ready to get serious but I'm not. I had plenty of time to think on it, and I came to that conclusion." Derell responded. Janae had given him a look that read she was heartbroken by his response. He halfway felt bad for her, but he had to be honest.

"Fuck ass," Lailah said under her breath.

"You had all that mouth earlier, you wanna share with the table?!" Derell raged. He knew Lailah's comment was pinpointed toward him.

"Yea. I said. FUCK ASS! Clown-ass nigga." Lailah fumed.

"Aye aye, chill out Lai. It's between him and Janae. Stay out of it." Zion said. The last thing he needed was the love of his life and his best friend beefing with each other.

"Whateva," Lailah shook her head and took a few bites from her calamari.

"Well I'm sorry you feel that way cause you're gonna have to deal with me after all." Janae took a long pause.

"Fuck you mean?" Derell's heart started to race.

"I'm pregnant." Janae answered. She looked at Derell's jaw dropping expression and almost busted out in laughter. She now had pure hate for Derell and didn't care to be with him anymore. Janae handled rejection like a child.

"Bitch, you's a lie. I wanna see some paperwork." Derell commented. Shocked was an understatement to describe how he felt in that moment. Janae grabbed her purse and took out two pieces of paper that was stapled together and handed them to Derell. He read the results that confirmed what Janae had already told him. He didn't have any intentions on being someone's father no time soon. "You sure it's mine?"

Whap!

Janae slapped Derell hard across his face. She was taken back and disgusted by the nerve of him making that accusation. "You a bitch-ass nigga to even ask me that! You may have still been fucking around, but I wasn't!" Janae got up and left with Lailah running behind her.

"This whole situation was foul as fuck." Derell complained, tossing the test results on the table.

"My nigga, I'm sorry. Had I known that they were plotting some gang up on you shit, I would have never invited you." Zion stated sincerely.

"I know brah, but you better watch that tag team shit. Next time, it might be you." Derell warned.

Zion didn't like the way Lailah had played her hand in gathering everyone together. He understood her loyalty to her best friend, but he was loyal to his too. If they were going to be married, she needed to understand that the little game she played on Derell was unacceptable and that he wasn't going for his wife being messy, not even for her best friend.

Zion, Kyron, Derell, and five other guys raised their glasses in the air as they downed their ninth shot. Derell threw together a last-minute kickback at his place and invited some females over as well. He didn't take the news too well of him becoming a father in seven months. Tonight, he wanted to forget about the argument he had with Janae and continue to drink his problems away. He puffed on the personal blunt he had between his fingers and stood beside his kitchen table, where a game of spades took place. He took his place back of being the scorekeeper when he gestured for his main bitch Simone to come over. Simone had a caramel skin-tone, small gap, was slender, and had a juicy ass. She rocked a deep wave frontal and wore boatloads of make-up, which Derell found attractive. Derell wrapped one of his arms around her waist and grabbed her ass. Simone gave Derell a kiss as she took the blunt and took a few hits. Derell looked over at Zion who was sitting on the couch and looked to be fucked up from all the liquor he consumed.

"Go and grab your friend." Derell instructed Simone. He

had a devious smile on his face as he went and got his remote from off his entertainment center.

"Aight." Simone replied.

"Aye, aye, aye. Attention y'alllll." Derell slurred. "My dude is getting married very soon, and I wanna grace him with a present." Derell guided Zion into a chair that was centered in the middle of the living room and pressed the button to his speaker. Lil Ru's *Nasty Song* began to play and a female walked seductively towards Zion as they both locked eyes. The female sat on top of Zion and grinded along with the music. The way she was moving her hips made Zion's dick get hard with a quickness. He was instantly attracted to her; regardless of how drunk he was, his vision was still clear. The female performed all types of splits and tricks on Zion that he never seen before. Derell, along with all the other dudes in attendance, had a front row seat to the lap dance that had their full attention. Derell smirked at Zion's reaction, who was enjoying every minute of his personal strip tease. The girl was light-skin, long silky brown hair, green eyes, thick thighs, and had a small waist. Zion couldn't help himself as the liquor took over when his hands groped over the ass that was in front of him.

"*Shit!*" Zion said to himself. He slapped the girl's ass as she twirled it around and around. Zion felt like she had to be a professional dancer the way she was moving. In between her dance, she was being a little rough and would grab Zion's head as she moved but Zion didn't mind. When the song ended, Zion took the girl by her hand and led her down a hallway.

Derell didn't stop Zion when he seen him disappear with the girl towards one of the spare bedrooms. It was going on four o' clock in the morning when Derell walked his guests to the door. He took a high Simone and left to go to his bedroom that was located on the opposite side of the house.

Meanwhile, Zion and the woman helped each other take off their clothes while kissing in between. Zion laid flat on his back as the female got on top and stroked his dick. She lubricated his thick member with her spit and began sucking and jacking him off at the same time.

"Fuckkkk yea." Zion grabbed her hair and started fucking her mouth. "Shittttt!!" The female began deep-throating his dick, taking all of him like the pro she was. Zion was moaning like a bitch at that point and didn't care. She sucked harder and faster until she felt Zion's cum fill her throat. "Damn!" Zion said out of breath.

The female hopped off the bed and went to spit out his load in the toilet. She then came back and seen Zion's eyes still closed but could tell he was still awake. She reached into her shorts pocket and Zion seen her pulling out a condom. When he closed his eyes again, the female took the condom out of its wrapper and quickly poked a hole at the top. She then slid the condom down on Zion's semi-hard dick and began riding it back to life. Zion held onto her hips as he enjoyed the pleasure he was receiving.

"Ohhh, dadddyyyyy!!" The girl moaned out. This was by far the best dick she had in a very long time. His stroke made her feel all types of ways and had her pussy creamier than ever.

"You like that shit? Huh?" Zion slapped her ass. He flipped her over onto her side and held up one of her legs as he gave her deep and slow strokes.

"Yesssssss!! Fuck this pussy!!. Right thereeee!!" The girl yelled. As Zion picked up his pace, she felt herself about to cum.

"Damnnnn, you got some good pussy." Zion muttered.

He had to give credit when it was due and the female before him was satisfying all his needs in that moment. Not once did Lailah come across Zion's mind, which was part of the reason why he was giving one of his best performances. Zion put the female in the doggy style position and was turned on by how deep she arched her back. He rammed his thick rod back inside her tight pink pussy and began pounding away.

"Fuckkkk!! I'm 'bout to cummmm!!" The girl screamed.

"Cum then." Zion ordered. He held onto the girl's shoulders as he found her spot. After a few more intense strokes, she then came hard on his dick as Zion released his seeds quickly after her. "What's ya name?" Zion asked as he laid down beside her.

"Kimani."

*I*t was 3:30 pm when Lailah got done with all her classes and left the library parking lot. Now that she was back in school, Lailah was already over the endless amount of assignments she had due. She drove over to Janae's apartment to help comfort her friend during her time of need. Janae had an abortion a few weeks after the fight she had with Derell at the restaurant and was still having a hard time coping. Lailah wanted nothing more than to be by her friend's side. When Lailah knocked on Janae's door, she could tell from Janae's puffy red eyes that she had been crying again.

"Hey girl," Janae greeted. She led Lailah to her living room and finished rolling up her blunt.

"Hey. What you been up to today?" Lailah asked. Her heart broke for her best friend because Janae's smoking habit had only increased. She didn't know what to say in order to make her friend feel any better.

"I just woke up before you got here. My life seems purposeless now." Janae said in a sad tone.

"Aye, don't say that. It was a tough decision for you to

make. Don't be so hard on ya self." Lailah replied. She rubbed Janae's shoulder as she watched a single tear come down her cheek.

"I know, it's like the shit is fucking me up every day now. I can only help but wonder how things would've been if I didn't go through with it. Would I have a girl or boy? Would I have been a good mother? When I told my parents, they were excited, which surprised the fuck outta me." Janae lit the end of her blunt and took a few hits. She then passed it over to Lailah, who declined at first but took part in the session anyway.

"Have you told them?"

"Yea, and they're disappointed in me. They kept saying how they would've helped me out and stuff. Which is all good and everything, but I wasn't trynna have them take care of my child. I already feel bad about them paying my bills now. You know?" Janae shook her head. Both her mind and her heart were telling her that she made the wrong decision.

"I feel what you saying. But you ain't gotta explain ya self to nobody. You did what you thought was the best option for you in the long run. And it's only between you and God." Lailah responded. She was one who was against abortions but understood Janae's reasoning in the matter.

"Yeaaa, you're right. That makes me feel a little bit better. But to be honest, as long as I live, Ion think I'ma ever get over it." Janae explained. She was an emotional wreck and had put half of the blame on Derell.

"And I don't expect you to. That's a heavy load to carry. You just gotta take it one day at a time cause you're not alone. What Derell had to say about it?" Lailah asked. She went into a small coughing spell, which made Janae chuckle. "Oh, that's funny huh?" she was glad to put a smile on her face.

"Sound like you dying over there. But I haven't told him

just yet. That fuck-ass nigga wasn't ready to be no one's father anyway." Janae spat.

"Hell yea. He had a lot of nerve the way he acted that night."

"Damn right he did. Besides him being a complete asshole and wanting to deny my baby in front of you and Zion. My thing about it is, don't fucking tell me that you want us to be together but switch up when one of your homeboys is around. Like fuck that shit! Who the fuck you trynna flex for? Like nigga, you ended up playing ya self."

"Right, nigga's just wanna have it all."

"Not with me. He should've never crossed that line period."

"Exactly."

"How you and the future mista?" Janae was irritated at the thought of Derell and wanted to change the subject.

"Yeaaaa, he's been working a lot more since classes started back, which is fine with me because my work gives me a good distraction from the shit he got going on."

"So you still upset over him dealing or what?"

"I mean, I still feel some type of way about it cause you know how that shit can go. I learned to accept it and he says he about to wrap it up in a few more months. But anything can go wrong within that amount of time."

"Well, try not to think like that. He's smart and he doesn't draw any attention to himself, so he should be good." Janae poured herself a shot of 1800 silver and took it to the head. "I still can't believe y'all getting married. Has he told you where y'all going for y'all's honeymoon?"

"No, and it's killing me. He wants it to be a surprise."

"I got another question. How'd you feel if you got preggo during your senior year?"

"I'd be a little bit scared cause I don't want any kids until I'm done with grad school. But IF it happened, I'd live with it and keep going." Lailah responded. Janae's question made her think because her and Zion never used any condoms. Lailah was on the pill but even that wasn't a guarantee that she wouldn't pop up pregnant.

"Aweee how sweet."

"Don't put that shit on me tho. You know my ass ain't ready yet." Lailah laid back and let the effects from the loud take over. It was like the stress from her classes had been wiped away with a quickness.

"Yea I know. Your mom reached out to you lately?"

"She's been calling and I been ignoring. I ain't got a damn thing to say to her. Her actions were loud and clear." Lailah shrugged. She didn't feel bad about giving her mother the cold shoulder. Lailah was tired of getting disappointed time after time again from Natalie.

"Right, right. So have you thought more about where you gonna go for graduate school?"

"Yea, and I made up my mind to go to Georgia State. And I was also thinking that you should come too. We all need a fresh new start. North Carolina ain't got shit for us out here. There's plenty of opportunities in Atlanta, so why not go? Plus the trio will be back together again." Lailah explained. The more she thought about her move to another state, the more excited she got. She desperately wanted Janae to go along with her but didn't know if she sounded convincing enough.

"You made some valid points but I'ma think on it."

"You have time, so there's no rush. If you wanna stay here and complete your bachelors, that's understandable too. Cause out-of-state tuition is a bitch."

"You mothafuckin' right. Shit is ridiculous is what it is. Government don't give a fuck."

"Which is a shame too. But fuck 'em. You need to get out

and get some fresh air. You down for some hibachi?" Lailah suggested.

"Yea, sounds good. What time you trynna go?"

"Whenever you get ready. But I invited a girl who's in my class and we became good friends. She transferred here her sophomore year and haven't gone out too much since being here. And I thought it would be good for you guys to meet. You fine with that?"

"Yea, it's no problem. I like meeting new people. Sometimes." Janae stated. She got up and went towards her bedroom to take a shower.

"Keyword *sometimes*." Lailah yelled after her. She reached down to pick up the remote from the table and searched through the channels. She finally came across the movie *Bad Teacher*, which was one of her favorite movies. Lailah only hoped the meeting with her classmate and Janae went well because she knew how protective Janae was over their friendship. Thirty minutes passed and Janae came back out to the living room. "Well don't you look cute." Lailah commented.

"Thank you." Janae smiled. She was wearing a white and navy top with light denim mom jeans and pair of tan Birkenstocks. "Where'd you have in mind to go?"

"Hiro's of course. We haven't ate there in a hot minute."

"Great minds think alike. You wanna ride with me or what?"

"Yea." Lailah said. She followed Janae outside and into her car.

Janae made the twenty-five-minute drive to the Japanese restaurant and pulled into the parking lot. They had made it just in time before the dinner rush and went inside where they got seated to their table.

"Where is she?" Janae questioned as she sat down. She looked over her menu and was pondering on what to order.

"Ion know but I'm 'bout to text her and tell her we're already here." Lailah replied. She took out her phone and seen a missed call from Zion and chose to hit him up later. "She's said she's turning in now."

"What class y'all take together?"

"It's a humanities course. Boring shit but our professor makes it interesting. Thank God. She's very cool and lenient, so it'll be an easy 'A.'"

"Is that her?" Janae asked as she saw a female approaching their table. As soon as Janae made close eye-contact with the female she instantly got a bad feeling.

"Yea, that's her." Lailah stood up and gave the female a hug and introduced her to Janae. "Janae, this is Kimani, Kimani, Janae."

"Nice to meet you," Kimani commented. She shook Janae's hand and recognized the death stare Janae was giving off.

"You too." Janae replied. There was something about Kimani that didn't sit well with Janae. Janae didn't know what it was but she would soon find out.

"You go to UNCW too Janae?" Kimani asked in a sassy tone. It was obvious that Janae didn't like her and the feeling became mutual.

"Nah, I went to Cape Fear and got my degree." Janae answered.

"Oh yea? Hmph. What you get your degree in?"

"Associate in Arts. What are you going for?" Janae mean-mugged. She was waiting for Kimani to say the wrong thing so she could pop off.

"Journalism. Can't afford to waste any time." Kimani provoked. She could tell she was getting under Janae's skin and didn't care.

"So you trynna be on the news or host some shit? Well

good luck with that, cause you gonna need it." Janae shot back.

"Oooookay! Have y'all ladies decided on what your gonna order?" Lailah interjected. She didn't understand where the sudden tension came from between Janae and Kimani. Lailah tried to be the peacemaker before things escalated any further.

"I understand it's quite hard to get a job with an Associate's degree. So tell us your secret on how you making it." Kimani dismissed Lailah's voice of reason. As far as she was concerned, Kimani felt like Lailah should have checked Janae for her attitude and rudeness.

"That's none of ya business." Janae spat.

"Mm. Must be nice to have mommy and daddy pay for everything." Kimani stated.

"Bitch, you don't know shit about me!" Janae stood up and yelled. She was close to smacking Kimani until Lailah got in the middle of both of them.

"Hey, hey, hey! Y'all stop! Janae, what the hell is wrong with you?! Y'all two just met! So what could possibly be the problem?!" Lailah ranted, looking back and forth between Janae and Kimani.

"That high yella bitch is the problem! Fuck her! I'm leaving. You coming?" Janae grabbed her purse and keys.

"I'll take you home Lailah since your so-called *friend* here is leaving you on stuck." Kimani commented. There was fire when she looked into Janae's eyes, but she was the least bit of intimidated. She had been in plenty of fights during her twenty-two years of being on this earth and Janae pumped no fear in her heart.

"Let me get outta here before I go to jail. Lailah call me if you need me. Cause I don't trust this bitch," Janae pointed at Kimani as she walked away.

"What the hell just happened? I mean, do y'all know each

other from the past or sum? I'm fucking lost." Lailah flopped back down into her chair feeling confused.

"Hell no. Let's not forget that yo friend started with me. For what? I don't know." Kimani replied. She didn't know what Janae's problem was with her and all she could pin it towards her being jealous of her looks.

"I apologize for her behavior. She's been going through a lot these past couple months." Lailah expressed. Their table then filled up with more customers as their waitress came over and took their orders.

"Mm. It's cool. Everyone has an off day sometimes. She's still old enough to know how to control herself." Kimani added. She wasn't pressed about becoming Janae's friend and felt their drama had just begun.

"Let's just enjoy the rest of the evening," Lailah stated. Lailah took Janae's statements and concerns serious because majority of the time, she was always right. She made a mental note to confront Janae about her ill feelings towards Kimani.

CHAPTER 27

"*I*'ve missed you soooooo much man." Zion expressed. Him and Lailah were snuggled up against each other on his hammock that was placed on his private balcony. It was a Saturday evening, and the temperatures were cool enough to enjoy the outside. With Zion living right beside the beach, they were graced with plenty of breezes from every direction.

"The lies you tell." Lailah joked. She was glad to be in Zion's strong arms. There was no other place she'd rather be in that moment.

"I'm forreal. Tell me how's school coming along."

"Getting on my damn nerves. I'm close to pulling every strand of my hair out." Lailah demonstrated with her fingers.

"Just hang in there a lil bit longer bae. You got it. But tell me when you gonna have me a junior?." Zion questioned. He had been nutting in Lailah for pleasure and on purpose to impregnate her for the longest.

"Damn, can I at least finish school first? You in a hurry or something?" Lailah said with an attitude. Zion's words made her feel like he was trynna trap her, even though they were close to being husband and wife.

"Nah, I'm was only asking baby. Chill. I can wait." Zion responded. He rubbed her soft booty and gave it a few slaps. "Is that roast almost done yet? You trynna starve a nigga and shit."

"It should be done now. I gotta go and check it. Hell, you the one that should be cooking for me."

"Is that right? I will. Just gotta tell me what you want." Zion bit his lip. He felt like shit knowing the secret he was keeping from her as he looked into her eyes. He had plans on telling her about his recent rendezvous but didn't know how to come out and say it. If Lailah left him, he wouldn't know how to handle it or move on with his life.

"Bullshit. Yo ass just wanna be lazy now. I'ma just go ahead and tell you to not get used to this shit. I work just as hard as you nigga, and I'm not obligated to come home and cook a full meal every damn day. So you can get that lil fantasy out yo head." Lailah explained. She was tired of the double standards that dudes had with females. She didn't care whether if Zion got upset or not, he needed to know how she felt.

"And I can respect that. You won't have no complaints from my end."

"Mhmm, you say that shit now." Lailah rolled her eyes. She took her time getting out the hammock and headed to the kitchen. Lailah took the lid from off the crockpot and checked to see if her meat was done. When she was satisfied with her results, she checked on her other sides as they were almost done cooking as well. She stirred up her cabbage and looked inside the oven at her macaroni and cheese. She smiled as she took two oven mitts and took out her home-made baked macaroni and set it on top of the island.

Ding Dong!

"I got it baby." Zion jogged to the door and let Kyron inside. They gave each other a brotherly embrace then joined Lailah in the kitchen, who was placing biscuits on a cookie sheet. "Bae, this is Kyron. My otha partner I told you about." Zion introduced.

"Wassup Kyron? Nice to finally meet you." Lailah gave Kyron a handshake. "How many biscuits you gone eat Kyron?"

"Three." Kyron answered. He was secretly checking out Lailah and could see the reason why she had Zion wide open and ready to marry her. He had seen a good number of pretty females, but Lailah's beauty was definitely one in a million.

"Aight, just give me like fifteen more minutes and everything will be done fellas." Lailah assured.

"Finally. But I'll be back bae. I gotta take this call." Zion said as he kissed her on the cheek and left out the room.

"So Kyron, you from round here?" Lailah asked in her country accent. She noticed the look he gave her once he first laid eyes on her and didn't know how to feel about it. Kyron was beyond sexy, which surprised Lailah because she didn't go for light-skin dudes. Kyron had hazel eyes, a low hair cut that exposed his deep waves, a full beard, and stood at 6'2.

"Nah, I'm originally from Virginia and came down here when I was twelve." Kyron said. He knew of Zion's recent infidelity and wanted to tell Lailah, but it wasn't his place. Everything would soon come to light and he would prepare himself before that time came. Lailah had his attention, and it would be a matter of time before he came in and took Zion's place.

CHAPTER 28

*Z*ion woke up to some morning head and fucked Kimani's mouth as she sucked him nice and slow. They had been fucking around ever since Derell's kickback. Zion told himself each time would be the last time, but it was easier said than done. He didn't have any feelings for Kimani, but he couldn't let go of the addictive sex they had. His heart was committed to Lailah, but his dick belonged to both Lailah and Kimani. He didn't understand how he got himself mixed back up in some bullshit. Zion made a promise to both him and Lailah that he would never fuck around, but now things have become more complicated than ever. Kimani loved to have rough sex where Zion would choke and throw her around whereas Lailah longed for deep passionate love-making. He had the best of both worlds, but he would soon have to end his affair with Kimani.

"Fuck yeaaa. Just like that. Sssssss," Zion moaned as he bit his bottom lip. Kimani was giving him some sloppy toppy as Plies Ft Pleasure P *Get You Wet* played in the background. Zion and Kimani messed around at her apartment that she shared with a college roommate. Zion couldn't risk bringing

Kimani to any of his places because he didn't know if she would turn into a stalker. Plus he would never have sex with her in the same bed as Lailah. "Shittttt!! I'm cuming!" Zion pumped faster as he released a huge load in her mouth. Kimani then got up and did her normal routine where she'd spit out his cum in the toilet and brushed her teeth afterwards. When she got back in bed, she went in for a kiss but Zion rejected her.

"What is it? My mouth is fine now." Kimani asked. She would never understand his reasoning to why he wouldn't kiss her. She turned off her music and turned on her TV. instead.

"Nah, you not mine. That's why." Zion answered. He didn't feel obligated to explain himself to Kimani. She had no business questioning him as far as he was concerned.

"Well I can be," Kimani smiled as she climbed on top of Zion. She ran her hands over his chest and planted soft kisses around his neck.

"We done talked about this. I like things the way they are. No need in messing up what we have going on." Zion pressed. In one swift motion, he moved Kimani off his lap and sat up on the side of the bed. Zion didn't tell her that he was in a relationship let alone engaged because he had no idea that their situation would end up lasting this long.

"Okay, so? What if I wanna talk about it?" Kimani snapped. She could tell that Zion was keeping something from her and decided to keep pressuring him until he told her what it was.

"You'd be setting ya self up. So I suggest you don't fucking go there." Zion fumbled for his clothes and began putting them back on. It was like Kimani was beginning to act like another Toree.

"Tell me! Is it because I'm a stripper? I don't fuck on the side for money like other bitches! I get paid enough from just being on stage and hosting shows at the club. That's it. Nothing else." Kimani explained. She felt something for Zion the night they first met and his sex game was a huge part of it as well.

"You think I wanna be with a girl who done showed her body off to every nigga?! The fuck?" Zion pushed Kimani out of his way as he reached for his shirt and sneakers. He had no patience to deal with Kimani's rant at the moment. He was now regretting ever getting involved with her.

"So what?! I'm paying my way through school cause a nine-to-five ain't gone cut it! At least give me some type of credit! Damn!" Kimani yelled. She was trying any and every-thing to get Zion to see her point of view but nothing was working.

"Why the fuck is you yelling? And I have. But there are plenty of people in college who work a nine-to-five and they're making it alright. So what's yo excuse? What? Cause you want fast money? What do you really get in the end besides a fucked-up reputation?" Zion shot back.

"And who the fuck are you nigga to be judging me for how I decide to make my money? As if your job is any better!" Kimani fumed. She was close to crying but refused to let any teardrop fall.

"You got a point there but still. I don't want a chick that's in the strip club. Sorry not sorry."

"What if I quit?! Would you still feel the same way?" Kimani questioned.

"Yep. Ain't shit you can do to change my mind. I already have someone that has the key to my heart." Zion confessed.

"Oh, so now you wanna tell me?! You's the definition of a true fuck-nigga! How long was you planning on keeping this from me?" Kimani pushed and punched Zion in the back and chest. She didn't realize how deep her feelings were for Zion until now.

"Back the fuck up before I hurt yo ass! I don't hit women, but I will tear a bitch ass up! Keep putting yo fuckin' hands on me!" Zion threatened. The seriousness in his voice made Kimani take a couple steps back and put space between them.

"And why does it matter? We were never going to be together, so I don't know wat'chu mad for. So kill all that shit you talking. But yes, I have a fiancée."

"Fiancée?!" Kimani could believe the words that just came out of his mouth.

"You heard me."

"Then why are you with me almost every night? Rolling around in my sheets, bussing my fucking guts?!" Kimani seethed.

"Cause the pussy good. End of story." Zion grabbed his keys and phone.

"Nah, nigga. You're sadly mistaken. It's never gonna be the end cause I'm *pregnant*." Kimani stated in a cold tone.

"What?" Zion looked back at Kimani. He felt his heart drop from the news she just shared but remained calm on the outside.

"You heard me," Kimani mocked. She been popping holes into every condom they used every time they had sex. After a month of trying, Kimani finally got knocked up.

"Whether it's mine or not, I recommend you get rid of it." Zion reached into his pocket and placed a band on Kimani's dresser and walked out before she could respond.

Zion got in his car and went to pay Kyron a visit. Usually, he would tell Derell all his skeletons, but this time he needed someone who was level-headed in his corner. He couldn't fathom the thought of Kimani being pregnant. His mind raced over to Lailah as his palms got sweaty while he drove. The betrayal he committed was eating away at his conscience. Zion couldn't get out his car fast enough when he got to Kyron's front door.

"Wassup man?" Kyron looked at Zion with concern. He stepped aside so Zion could walk in.

"I need to talk to you brah." Zion replied. He sat down in one of Kyron's chairs in the living room and ran his hands down over his face in frustration.

"Here man… from the looks of things, you need this more than me right now." Kyron handed him the freshly rolled blunt and went into his kitchen to bring back two shot glasses and a bottle of Patron. "It gotta be some heavy shit for you to be acting like this."

"Heavy ain't even the word man. But you not gonna believe this shit." Zion took a few puffs from the blunt and allowed the smoke to fill his lungs. He took a long pause before telling his story.

"Shit, did somebody die or sum?" Kyron was now getting a little impatient as he begun to roll up again.

"Nah. Kimani's ass is pregnant." Zion admitted. Hearing those words made him want to vomit. He couldn't believe this was his life right now.

"Who the fuck is Kimani?" Kyron looked confused. The name sounded familiar, but it still wasn't registering to him. The fact that it wasn't Lailah made him happy.

"The bitch that was at Derell's crib that night. Member?" Zion explained.

"Ohhh, okay. Yea, I remember. Wayment, what nigga?" Kyron pretended to be surprised. He knew that Zion's old ways would catch up to him. It was just sad that Lailah was the true sufferer in the end.

"She just told me the shit. We been fucking around for almost three months now. Shit crazy dude. Her ass trapped me on purpose." Zion ranted. He had the look of evil in his eyes and had a million of different scenarios going through his head.

"Well did y'all ever go raw one time?" Kyron questioned.

"And that's the thing! I made sure to use protection every fucking time man! Every time!"

"Well if that's the case, it's probably a possibility that it ain't yours then." Kyron took out his phone and made a call to order him some pizza; he asked Zion if he wanted anything and ordered him something as well. "Okay, but back to the convo, yea man. Just get a test."

"Fuck alla that. I wish it was that simple. I'm positive her ass wasn't fucking with no one else but me. And how I know is cause we got into an argument over us becoming a couple," Zion shook his head. He started to get the chills over the situation he was now in with Kimani.

"Well damn. What the fuck you be doing to these girls man?" Kyron said.

"Not shit. After I told her about Lailah, that's when her ass went crazy. Hitting me and all types of shit. But I quickly put that bullshit to an end."

"So what you gonna do?" Kyron asked.

"I don't know man, that's why I came to you. I couldn't ask D cause him and Janae got they own problems going on. She's pregnant too." Zion informed.

"Shut the fuck up." Kyron looked at Zion in suspense.

"Hell yea." Zion answered. He watched Kyron go to the door and pay for their food. He brought their boxes over to the table where they were seated and went into the kitchen to get a couple of paper plates.

"D ass bout to become somebody's daddy? That'll be a sight to see. Wonder will that make his ass finally grow the fuck up." Kyron commented. He could say that Derell was a good partner when it came to them working but outside of that, he acted like a little kid at times.

167

"What I'm gone do Ky? I don't wanna lose Lai. It'll tear us apart."

"I don't see no other option but for you to tell her. I know that's not what you wanna hear, but there's no other way around it. Either you tell her or she's gonna end up hearing it from someone else, which will only make it worse. So it's best you tell her." Kyron replied. He knew that once this information got back to Lailah, things between them would never be the same. It would surprise Kyron if Lailah ended up staying with Zion after hearing the news. She didn't seem like the type of female who was weak-minded.

"Fuck! I don't know when I'ma tell her. I even gave Kimani some money for an abortion. Her ass betta do it." Zion stated. He took a few bites from his cheese pizza and thought more on Kyron's advice.

"Is that how you really feel? Or you just pissed because it's Kimani rather than Lailah?"

"Shit, both." Zion replied. He was starting to overthink his situation and felt a small headache approaching.

"You still going through with the wedding?" Kyron wondered how things would go between Zion and Lailah after they got married.

"Hell yea. I wrote out my vows and everything. Lailah is my heart man. I know I fucked up and I'm praying that she'll forgive me. I don't know what I'd do without her." The conversation he had with Lailah about her ex kept replaying in his head over and over again. There was a strong possibility that Lailah wouldn't forgive him.

"So tell me, how'd you end up continuously fucking Kimani?"

"I ain't gonna lie… that bitch a freak and it was hard to let her go. She was way better than Toree's ass."

"And Lailah?"

"Nah, they tied." Zion answered.

"Okay then, so lemme ask you this. Let's say Kimani didn't get pregnant, would you continue to fuck with her even after marrying Lailah?"

"That's a hard question only because I planned on ending shit with Kimani a long time ago."

"That didn't answer my question. So I'ma take that as a no since you had 'plans' but couldn't bring ya self to stop." Kyron respected Zion as a boss, but it was guys like him that he couldn't stand that would fuck over a good female. He knew that Zion was never going to do right by Lailah and here it was that it didn't take long.

"Kimani strips for a living brah. Even if she did stop stripping and chose to work a regular job, I still wouldn't cuff her ass. She's fine and all, but I love my sexy chocolate. Don't no other woman measure up to my Lai."

"Then why continue to fuck Kimani?"

"I guess I fooled myself into thinking that I could be a one-woman-man. And I really felt like I could and that I was ready. The crazy part about all this shit is that my mom called it when I went to go visit her."

"Forreal?"

"Yea, man. Sadly, she turned out to be right. Which fucks me up inside cause she didn't even raise me to know about my personality or none of that shit." Zion stated.

"Do the right thing. She deserves to know brah. Don't wait until the last minute."

OCTOBER 18TH

*I*t was finally the day of Zion and Lailah's wedding as the men and women were in separate rooms getting ready. The temperature was perfect on the island and Zion felt everything was going as planned. Kyron fixed his bow-tie and could sense Zion's nervousness.

"You ready to do this?" Kyron asked as he looked in the mirror at Zion.

"Of course man. I'm marrying the woman of my dreams in less than thirty minutes. I just want everything to be perfect." Zion huffed. His heart was beating a mile a minute as he felt butterflies in his stomach. He couldn't wait to see Lailah walking down the aisle and to finally become her husband. Thoughts of Kimani's pregnancy was now a distant memory as he focused on Lailah and Lailah only. After the ceremony, Zion made plans for him and Lailah to fly straight to their honeymoon as he paid for the rest of the wedding party to stay in St Lucia. Lailah was on her fall break and gave in to missing an extra day of class, so they could spend more time together on their getaway.

Zion, Kyron, and Derell made their way outside and took

their places on the pier. After a few minutes, Janae and Olivia joined them. Janae had a microphone and began singing Leela James' *Fall For You*. All the men were shocked to hear Janae's angelic voice because they didn't know she could sing. Once Janae got to the middle of her song, everyone turned and watched Lailah slowly make her way down the walkway. Lailah had on a white Vera Wang strapless mermaid wedding dress, her hair was straightened, and was styled into wand curls. There was a veil covering her face, but Zion could tell she was crying underneath as a few tears escaped from his eyes as well. On cue, Lailah got to the finish line as Janae sung her last note. Since Zion and Lailah chose to have a short ceremony, the preacher wasted no time as he asked Zion and Lailah to recite their vows to each other. Zion decided to go first and said, "To be standing here with you today is like a dream come true. You give me hope. You brought the color into my world. I was lost, deep in sorrow because I didn't know what love was… that is until you came into my life and showed me the definition of true love. God knew what he was doing when he brought you to me. You make my life worth living. I want to continue to grow with you until the end of time. I thank God for you every day. I love you baby." Zion said as he held Lailah's hands.

"I was terrified to love again, but you came and took that fear away. You make my heart smile and melt at the same time. You bring light to my soul. I can't imagine life without you. You're my prince charming who saved me when I was close to falling into despair. Your patience with me is so amazing and I thank you for that. You're my sunshine whenever I'm having a bad day. I thought God had given up on me until I met you. The love we have is indescribable and I'm ready to take on this long journey with you and only you. I love you Zi." Lailah professed.

"By the power invested in me, I now pronounce you

husband and wife. You may salute your bride." The preacher announced.

CHAPTER 30

*L*ailah held baby Mia as she smiled for the picture along with Olivia standing by her side. Lailah and Olivia's mom, Rachael, surprised Olivia with a baby shower back in North Carolina. They were also celebrating Olivia's new job at the hospital as an ICU Nurse. Zion had paid for all the expenses that went towards Olivia's baby shower. Lailah did an outstanding job with the decorations and went above and beyond. It was an elephant theme with the colors pink, white, and grey. The location took place in a building that was close to the ocean and had an outside deck attached, where more photos were being taken. There was one table that held fifteen different varieties of food, and another table that displayed a wide spread of desserts. In attendance, there were a total of fifty guests that included: friends, family, and colleagues. The vibe was filled with tons of laughter and joyful conversations.

"She is toooo precious Liv!" Lailah commented. She looked down at Mia who was busy sucking her pacifier. Lailah fell in love the first moment she saw Mia and was ecstatic when Olivia made her the Godmother. "She's such a good baby."

"Thank you. And yea she is. Thank God. She only fusses when she's hungry and sometimes when she fights sleep. Other than that, I have no problems." Olivia replied.

"You making me want one now."

"Oh really? I'll be waiting." Olivia chuckled. She loved motherhood and wouldn't trade it for the world but at the same time it was a hard job.

"Tell me about y'all's honeymoon. Where he end up taking you?"

"Girl, Thailand! It was such a fun and amazing experience. We rode the elephants in the water and took pictures with them. They were so sweet. Next time, me, you and Janae gotta go." Lailah stated. She reminisced back on her and Zion's trip and was sad that it been cut short.

"I'm jealous. But I'm glad you had a great time. And how is Janae doing?" Olivia was recently informed by Janae about her abortion and saddened by the news. Janae decided not to attend Olivia's baby shower for obvious reasons and Olivia didn't hold it against her.

"She's trying to make it, but she hasn't been the same since. It's been killing her in the inside. And me, I feel so helpless because I don't know what to say or do to make her feel better." Lailah explained. It broke her heart to see her friend in such misery and how Janae would now smoke and drink herself to sleep. Lailah was starting to worry about Janae's health and made a mental note to bring it up the next time she saw her.

"Well with that particular subject, there's only so much you can say or do. It's a touchy and emotional-scarring situation. But keep being there for her. You're doing the right thing." Olivia said.

"And I will." Lailah handed over baby Mia to Olivia so she could get fed.

"Do you still breastfeed?"

"Girl no. I gave up after four days." Olivia answered. She gave her daughter the rest of her bottle and kissed her on the cheek.

"Why?" Lailah laughed. She took a bite from one of her strawberry cupcakes.

"That crap hurt! Honey, I give props to our ancestors and other women who do it today. Plus with my job it wouldn't have worked out anyway. With me working twelve hour shifts complicates things."

"Oookay. Got'chu. How you liking it so far?"

"I like it cause there's always something for me to do. It's very fast paced and the checks ain't bad eitha." Olivia now put her daughter across her shoulder and patted her back until she heard a burp. "Good girlll." Olivia rubbed Mia's tiny back. "How does it feel to be married?"

"Honestly, to me, no different. We just have another title. Maybe to him, he may feel a difference. Also, I thought it was gonna be a nightmare living with him, but he loves to clean up as much as I do."

"Well did he ever give you any reason to think he was a slob or sum?"

"No but you know how niggas can act one way in the beginning and turn out to be the complete opposite once y'all move in together."

"True true. Where's your dress?"

"Hanging up in its own display box. That dress ran him sixty bands."

"Shittt. That was nothing but chump change to him tho."

"Hell yea. How was your stay in the Caribbean?" Lailah reached for Mia and rocked her to sleep.

"I'm ready to go back. The beach was my favorite part. The crystal-clear waters and the white sand was just beautiful. I see why you loved it so much and chose to get married there, that place is wonderful. Me and Janae went out to the club and met some of the dudes there and had fun. We never really associated with Kyron and Derell until it was time for us to leave."

"When's the last time you talked to Irvin?"

"Like almost a month ago. He only seen her twice since she's been born. It's whateva, I ain't gone force him to do shit. I make enough money to take care of me and her, so I don't need a damn thing from him really. What I'm upset about is how niggas can make a baby and have the luxury to walk away from their responsibilities. But us females, we get stuck having to play both roles and don't have a choice in the matter. That's what kills me."

"It's sad and pathetic and it's not fair or right." Lailah agreed. She felt sorry for her friend and her having to be a single mom but knew that Olivia was strong enough to move on. She looked down at Mia who was sleeping peacefully in her arms.

"You're a natural Lai." Olivia watched how gentle Lailah was with her daughter. "You're gonna be a good mother one day."

"I hope so."

"You will. And thank you for putting this together. You did an amazing job. Me and Mia appreciate everything you do for us."

"No problem girl. I had fun planning it I must say. Yo mama is a trip. I forgot how funny she was. She was talking mad shit about Irvin's ass. Had my stomach hurting."

"That's her. Between her and my dad, they take turns watching Mia and I'm thankful for them."

"Do they talk to each other still or no?"

"Nope. Only 'hey' and 'bye' is as far as it goes." Olivia

replied. Her parents got divorced when she was seven, due to Olivia's dad being a workaholic. Even into her adult years, her parent's separation still bothered her.

"Well at least they can be cordial with one another." Lailah said.

"Yeaaa. It still sucks tho that they couldn't work things out. It damaged my childhood." Olivia admitted. She didn't have any siblings to turn to or a shoulder to lean on.

"I see what you're saying sis. You ready to open your gifts?" Lailah asked. She got up with Mia in her arms and led Olivia to the front of the room where two chairs were present. Lailah took one seat as Olivia took the other. Olivia's eyes got wide as she was presented with all her gifts that her guests brought. Olivia received tons of clothes, shoes, accessories, and baby furniture from her shower. Along with footing the bill, Zion also paid for professionals to clean up afterwards once the baby shower was over.

AFTER SPENDING some extra time with Olivia and her family before they got on the road in the next few days, Lailah didn't get home until a little after 10 pm that night. Zion was still out handling business and told Lailah he wouldn't be home until around midnight. She had plans on surprising Zion before he got home, so she took this time to roll up and watch TV. to kill some time. An hour flew by when Lailah awoke from a quick nap and went upstairs to take a shower. After washing her hair and feeling rejuvenated, Lailah slipped into a blue alloy strappy chaffon lace babydoll lingerie. As she walked back downstairs, she saw Zion walking through the door.

"Shit, you looking sexy as fuck." Zion greeted as he met

Lailah at the bottom step. He picked her up and cupped her ass cheeks.

"All for you daddy." Lailah flirted. She kissed Zion on the lips as he carried her to the sofa.

"How did it turn out?"

"Great, everything was perfect. The food was delicious. Olivia and the rest of the guests had a good time. Nobody had any complaints. We took millions of pictures. Look." Lailah scrolled through her gallery and showed Zion some photos.

"She's beautiful." Zion commented. He looked at a photo with Lailah holding baby Mia that tugged at his heart. It only gave him thoughts about the family he would make with Lailah. "She has a lot of hair too."

"Mhmm. She took after her momma with everything. She definitely gives me baby fever."

"Oh yea? So don't you think we should start practicing?" Zion looked at Lailah with lust in his eyes. He gripped Lailah's ass as he felt himself getting hard.

"Slow ya roll tiger." Lailah laughed. She now knew she couldn't keep mentioning anything about having a baby to Zion because he would be hot and ready while Lailah wasn't up to having any kids yet.

"You gone get enough of interrupting me and him." Zion said.

"Y'all both will be just fine." Lailah rolled her eyes. She relit the blunt she had earlier and took a few puffs before handing it to Zion.

"I fucking beg to differ. But wassup? Tell me what's on yo mind." Zion questioned.

"You tell me. How are you enjoying the married life?" Lailah wanted to make sure that they were both on the same page.

"Shit, I'm loving it. It's a beautiful thing. No lie. I don't know why other niggas be so afraid of getting married. It ain't bad like they think."

"Me and almost every other female can answer that." Lailah said in a sarcastic tone.

"Enlighten me." Zion replied as he blew out a huge cloud of smoke. The way Lailah was looking made it hard for him to concentrate on their conversation.

"Because they're afraid they gonna miss out on sum shit. Different pussy. But it's like grow the fuck up already and put that shit to rest. Us females go through the most shit, so why should we have to wait on y'all for anything? That bachelor shit is tired."

"Damn, is that how you really feel? Sound like you got a lot of hostility built up. You good?"

"Yea, I'm just telling the truth on how it is. I speak for every real ass female out there who's ready for niggas to stop playing games and settle down." Lailah stated.

"Well, you got a real ass nigga here." Zion pulled Lailah in for another kiss. "Hell, you could be a spokesperson the way you sounding."

"And you and Derell would be my first guests."

"He apologizes by the way."

"And tell him he can keep that apology." Lailah fumed.

"Why?"

"Fucking weak to send an apology through you. He can say it to my face, so I can see if it's sincere or not."

"He's going through a lot right now bae. Cut him a lil bit of slack."

"I wish the fuck I would. He doesn't get any special treatments. Janae is going through some shit as well." Lailah defended. If it wasn't for the loud she was smoking on, her attitude would have been a lot worse.

"What's your issue with him? Huh?" Zion questioned. He

was tired of the back and forth bickering between Derell and Lailah.

"I just don't like the fact of him trynna play Janae for a fool. That's my *issue*. He was telling you one thing and going back telling Janae another. Then when it was all said and done, he made her look stupid! And I don't respect him for that. Then he had the audacity to question their baby? Get the fuck outta here Zi. C'mon."

"Okay, okay. Maybe y'all two can talk at a later time. I can't stand seeing y'all bumping heads and shit." Zion professed. Lailah and Derell's beef was the least of his problems compared to the situation he had with Kimani.

"Yea I guess." Lailah placed the roach in her ashtray that was on the table.

Zion picked her up and headed upstairs without saying another word. When they made it to their bedroom, there was many lit candles around the room. Zion laid Lailah on top of their bed and went over to turn on his stereo system. Usher's *Can You Handle It* began to play as Zion crawled on top of the bed and guided himself between Lailah's legs. He carefully took off every piece of Lailah's lingerie and threw it on the floor. Zion laid on top of Lailah and kissed her while using his index finger to play with her clit. He teased her by making his finger go up and down around her wet opening.

"Ziiiii..." Lailah moaned. She wanted to feel his soft fingers go inside her but he wouldn't budge.

"This what you want?" Zion stuck his index finger into her tight box and played around until he found her spot. "Hmmm?"

"Yesssss baby!" Lailah squirmed around but couldn't go very far because Zion held her thighs both in place.

"Why you running?" Zion smiled. He went down and opened up Lailah's fat pussy lips and began slurping and eating her pussy like he hadn't had a meal in weeks. He loved the way Lailah tasted and looked up and made eye contact while he ate.

"Fuckkk!" Lailah moaned. She was close to cuming in his face as she tried to push his head away. Zion kept licking at her special spot until she busted in his mouth. "Shittt!" Lailah yelled. She watched Zion take off the rest of his clothes until he became fully naked. He opened Lailah's legs wider as he stuffed his dick inside her hotbox. "Ohhhhh! Zi!" Lailah cried out as he made deep strokes and groaned in her ear.

"You feel so fucking good baby." Zion whispered in her ear. He then placed both of Lailah's legs up to her head as he dug into her pussy.

"Fuckkk!! Oh my. . . . . Shitttt!" Lailah yelled. The way Zion was punishing her pussy had her going crazy.

"You like this shit?" Zion said as he pumped in and out.

"Yesssss!!" Lailah screamed. She was on the verge of having another orgasm, but Zion flipped her over as Lailah took control and rode his dick the way he liked.

"Work that shit baby." Zion commented. He slapped Lailah on the ass and put one of his arms behind his head. She was giving him a perfect view of her smooth chocolate ass as she glided up and down his nine inches.

"Mmmmm. I'm 'bout to cum!" Lailah shouted.

"Cum baby," Zion said. He held onto both her hips and fucked her back.

"Ohhhhhh!!! Don't stop!! Fuckkkkkkkk!!" Lailah tilted her head back in ecstasy as she came on Zion's thick member.

"Ahhhh!" Zion kept stroking until he came as well. He pulled Lailah up towards him as they gave each other kisses.

"I love you." Zion said, looking into Lailah's eyes.

"I love you more."

CHAPTER 31

*L*ailah looked over the worksheet their professor handed out and began looking up the answers from her textbook. She was halfway through the semester and was ready for winter break to roll around. Her classmate Kimani had missed a few days and came inside the class a few minutes late. Kimani took her seat next to Lailah and asked if she missed anything important.

"You ain't miss too much girl. All we been doing is reading chapters and had class discussions over what we read. We do have a test coming up in two days, and it's fifty questions. Half multiple-choice and half true or false." Lailah explained.

"Of course. I'm ready for this semester to be over already." Kimani sighed.

"You ain't neva lied." Lailah concurred. The amount of assignments she had due was stressing her out more than ever. The support she had from Zion and her friends was enough to keep her going.

"So how was the wedding?" Kimani asked. Lailah didn't

share too many personal details about her love life to Kimani but the basics.

"Gorgeous. We went over to Thailand for our honeymoon. And we made plans to go to Puerto Rico next month." Lailah didn't care to go deep into her marriage with Kimani because it was none of her business to know. They were only good friends within their class and were beginning to help build a stronger friendship.

"Sounds exciting! I found the answer to number six and eight." Kimani pointed out in her book. "Who ever made this course needs to be shot and they momma."

"Hell yea, cause I ain't neva gonna use this in my career. Ever. How's things going with you and yo dude?"

"Girl, this nigga told me to kill our baby."

"Oh my God! No! What the fuck? How heartless can you be?" Lailah shook her head.

"Right! That shit still got me speechless. I don't know what's his deal. But he got me all the way fucked up." Kimani spat.

"Well who is this nigga? Tell me. He goes here with us?"

"Nah, girl. He's a mad hustler. Talking money out the ass girl."

"Damn, I wonder if I've ever heard of him." Lailah thought thinking of Derell. *He probably knocked another one up then tried to back down.* She thought, shaking her head.

"I don't know, have you? His name is Zion..."

To be continued...